AWAKENING GODDESS

A Guardians of Terra Novel

R.N. GOSSER

To Jacque, who helped me develop and write this story: I couldn't have finished this novel without you!

To my beta readers: Thank you for reading my story, taking a chance on me, and offering some wonderful advice.

To my husband: Thank you for your unfailing support in me and my dreams.

First edition January 2022

Content Editing by: Sugar Free Editing

Interior Design by: Sugar Free Editing

Cover art by: Maria Christine Pagtalunan (Artscandare Book Cover Design)

Facebook.com/R.N.Gosser

Instagram.com/r.n.gosser

PROLOGUE

Death stood on the grassy knoll overlooking a graveyard. The black, smoke-riddled air threatened to choke his lungs. If he were a mere mortal, it might have succeeded.

He peered below and beheld thousands of mutilated bodies. They were strewn about haphazardly, as if a beast had rampaged and ravaged them. A head there, a body here, a foot somewhere far apart. He could still taste the metallic tinge of blood in the air, though the battle had been hours ago.

Death thought about the scene and felt nothing. He knew he should be disgusted, grief-stricken, or even sad. But he felt absolutely nothing. He contemplated the battleground and who must have created it.

Zeus. King of the gods.

Zeus was angry with the one who called himself the One True God. That was no secret. How long had he been building an army against the Christian god? Centuries? Millenia, perhaps?

Death didn't care to keep track of time, for he was older than time itself.

When the Christian god came to be those centuries ago, Zeus had seethed with rage. His humans had stopped praying to him. Soon, they stopped believing in him entirely.

That was the source of his real anger.

The more the humans ceased to worship Zeus, the weaker he became. And the more frantic and desperate he became. When Death thought about it this way, the battle made sense. Zeus had to act soon because he feared he would lose his powers entirely, although this was unheard of.

The thousands of humans, gods, and angels should not have died that night. Their deaths were in vain. All because of that childish Zeus.

Death had doubtless days of work ahead of him because it was his job to escort the souls to their final resting places. Until then, these souls would sit and wait in the dark nothingness. That should have stirred some emotion in him. But no. He still felt nothing.

If Zeus continued down this path—this endless quest for vengeance—there would be no more humans. No more gods, angels, or demons. The world would change for the worse, and that thought finally stirred an emotion within Death.

Yes, he mused.

He felt something. What was it? Anger? Yes, that was it. He was angrier than Cronus at this Zeus. The audacity to kill them—*all of them*—just because they no longer believed in him.

Zeus didn't have the authority to decide when souls would die. That was for Death alone to determine. Not even the almighty gods were safe from Death's cold embrace. If Zeus had his way, there would be no more life or death, nothing more to collect. Death himself would cease to exist, fading into the void, along with his powers.

That he could not tolerate.

No, he wouldn't stand idly by and allow the destruction of the delicate balance he created. Death was older than all these imbeciles combined, and he certainly wouldn't tolerate any of them deciding his fate.

Death would do something he had never done before. He was joining the war.

And he would win.

CHAPTER ONE

LIR

Lir sat at his cherrywood desk, filled with longing as he gazed out at the sea. He would give anything to be out there. Instead, he was cooped up in his office, doing tedious paperwork. Part of leading the Guardians of Terra included mundane shit like taxes and documentation of events. Lir missed the good old days when he could kill things and walk away, event over. It wasn't so simple now.

Humans were continuously evolving, always changing their ways. That now included electronics, something Lir despised. He growled at his computer as he continued entering numbers for the goddamn taxes on something called a "spreadsheet."

Alex burst through the door, sending a vase of flowers shattering to the ground. Jari had insisted they made the place look homey. Whatever that meant.

"We got a problem," Alex said, stepping over the broken glass and heading to his desk.

Lir looked up from his computer and glanced at his

second in command. The god of war wore his usual scowl, his amber eyes blazing with their typical intensity. Battle gear adorned his muscular frame.

Lir scrubbed a hand down his face, yet another headache lingering behind his eyelids. "What is it?" he grumbled.

Alex threw a newspaper article on his desk, sending a spray of dust everywhere.

"What? You want me to read this shit?" Lir picked up the paper with a sigh.

Alex cocked a grin. "Of course not. We both know you can't read."

Lir raised one brow.

"If you'll look at the article, you'll see what I'm talking about in big, bold letters." Alex pointed at the paper.

DO DEMONS REALLY EXIST?

Lir tapped a pen on his desk and glanced at the article, not reading it. He could read, despite Alex's rude remark, but he wasn't about to waste his precious time doing it. "What is this about?" he asked as he threw the newspaper back on the desk.

Alex paced the small room and ran a hand through his dark brown hair. "A group of demons attacked a local diner somewhere in middle-of-fucking-nowhere America. We need to get down there and check it out."

Lir returned his gaze to his monitor. "The local cops probably already cleaned it up and blocked it off from the public." He pinched the bridge of his nose while he spoke.

"Some caution tape isn't going to stop a group of gods from getting in. Besides, this has Zeus written all over it. The question is, why is he attacking a diner? It makes no sense. It's not public enough and he only killed"—Alex looked at the newspaper—"five people."

Lir stopped rubbing his temples and looked up at Alex. "That *is* weird. He wouldn't waste his resources on a small diner."

"That's why I'm bringing this to your attention, o wise one," Alex said, bowing deeply.

"Let's check it out then." Lir stood, stretched, and grabbed Claíomh Solais, his beloved sword. It gleamed in the dark, and even better, it never ran out of ammo.

He followed Alex through the portal and stepped down into the diner a moment later. His feet slipped on the crimson-stained tile.

He glanced around at the unimpressive, dingy diner. One of the small windows had been smashed in. Some cheap vinyl chairs had been thrown around, and a few lay broken on the floor. Lir scrunched his nose. The room smelled like blood, dead bodies, and poorly cooked food.

Why would Zeus send demons to attack this place?

Alex stepped over a dead body and rolled it over with his toe. "They're all women. Worse . . . the demon scumbags ate their tits." Alex pointed to the woman's chest, as if Lir couldn't determine her boob was missing by looking at her.

"We're probably dealing with a demon of lust or glut-tony," Lir said. "They like breasts because of the tissue."

"Oh, I can understand why they like breasts, Lir. Just not the eating them part." Alex grimaced as he checked another dead, boobless woman.

Something vibrated in Lir's pocket. He reached down and pulled out his cell phone with a scowl. *How do I answer this thing again?*

Alex saved him by pressing his thumb on the green button.

Ah, that's how.

"Hello?" a man's voice said.

Lir placed it against his ear and cleared his throat. "Yes. Hello. This is Lir, god of the sea, and leader of the Guardians of Terra." He gave the entire auspicious name, just in case.

The voice on the other end overflowed with authority. "This is Lieutenant General Johnson of the U.S. Army. I was told to reach out to you for assistance."

"That's correct. What can I do for you?"

"We received an anonymous phone call a while back, alerting us to a potential threat in Wyoming. One of my soldiers was sent out to assess this threat. It turned out to be a petite female. We didn't see a reason to alert you at the time—"

"Get to the point, General," Lir said, cutting off the commander mid-speech.

The Lieutenant General did not falter, and continued as if Lir had not interrupted him. The man had balls. Lir could respect that. He could recall few military commanders who held his respect—the list was very short—and this man had added himself to their ranks without even knowing it. Lir let him continue and waited patiently until a word caught his attention.

Goddess, the General had said.

"Wait? What about a goddess?" Lir interrupted.

The General sighed. "We were told by the anonymous caller that she is a goddess—"

"Wait. The woman in Wyoming is a goddess?"

"Yes. That's what I said." The General's voice held a note of impatience.

Lir laughed dryly. "That's not possible. The anonymous caller is pulling your leg, General. I know of all the gods and goddesses, and there are none located in Wyoming. My knowledge of the gods is up-to-date and thorough. I even know of the gods in hiding."

8

"At first, that was my belief as well, but . . ." He cleared his throat before continuing. "Well, there's a demon watching her, sir."

Lir's entire body came to attention. "What? Are you sure it's a demon?"

The Lieutenant General scoffed. "My soldier described a creature straight out of an H. P. Lovecraft novel, complete with red skin and gnashing teeth. You tell me what the hell that sounds like!"

Lir sighed. He didn't need this shit right now. "Alright, fine. As soon as I have time, I'll check on this woman and find out if she is, in fact, a goddess."

The General's irritation was evident as he spoke again. "I'm calling you now because she is in danger. The demon is already outside her place of employment. My soldier can't do anything against a demon, sir. You need to head out there. Now."

Lir growled into the phone. "Why did you waste so much time talking, you imbecile?" He removed the commander from his mental list of respected individuals.

"I had to give you all the information," the General growled back.

"Fine! Tell me where she is!" Lir yelled.

Once he'd received the coordinates, Lir stuffed the phone back into his pocket without hanging up. "Finish checking this out," he said to Alex. "I gotta go."

Alex cocked an eyebrow and waved him off. "Fine."

Lir nodded and jumped through the portal. Even if she wasn't a goddess, he wouldn't leave this woman without protection. He just hoped he would get there in time to save her.

CHAPTER TWO

MYA

Mya wiped the sweat off her forehead as she stood in the shitty little hotbox her boss called the kitchen. "Table one is complaining about the runny eggs," she said. She stared at the cook, waiting for him to respond. He would likely say something along the lines of, *Table one can shove my eggs up their ass.*

"There ain't nothin' wrong with my eggs," Eric said.

Close enough, she thought. *Just not the angry, violent part. Guess that was all me.*

"Come on, Eric." Mya pushed out her lower lip. "Just make them some new eggs. It'll take two seconds, I promise."

Eric slammed the pan onto the stove and turned to glare at her. "I don't got two secs to make 'em some new eggs, Mya! I got three other orders, and the place is swamped. You go make 'em some damn eggs."

"Right. Three orders must be total chaos." She rolled her eyes when he didn't respond and huffed as she walked to the fridge. She had all the time in the world to be a waitress *and* a cook. "Thanks for all your help, Eric!"

He still didn't respond.

She was so fed up with her life. This was where growing up as an orphan, running away from your abusive ex-boyfriend, and being poor got you: stuck in the middle of bum-fuck Nowhereville, Wyoming, working as a waitress making two bucks an hour. She longed for a different life. One of adventure, love, and financial freedom—all the things every other woman or man on Earth dreamed of. She sighed at that and slipped into a daydream about her knight in shining armor as she cooked the eggs.

The smell of burning rubber hit her nostrils and revived her from her self-pitying thoughts. "Crap," she whispered. Something told her this customer didn't appreciate burned eggs any more than undercooked ones. She snatched them off the burner and hoped for the best.

She walked to the overweight trucker sitting at table one. "Here are your eggs, sir. A fresh new batch! I hope they're to your satisfaction." She flashed a cheeky smile that she hoped would earn her a tip.

He simply grunted and started eating his new eggs.

If he cared that little, why complain in the first place? She walked away before she let her temper ruin her day further.

"Ma'am?" said a kid with dyed black hair and too much eyeliner.

She hated being called ma'am. She wasn't some gray-haired little old lady. She took another breath, hefted her tray in one hand, and headed to his table. "Yes?"

"Can I have the check, please?" He jerked his head to the side to shift the thick curtain of black hair from his eyes.

"Sure thing." She pulled the check out of her apron and

handed it to him. "Do you need anything else, sir?" See how he liked it.

"No, Ma'am. Thank you," he said.

She forced another smile. "Have a nice day!" she said, as sweetly as she could muster with the fake smile plastered across her face. *He better leave a fat tip.*

The rest of the night dragged on, boring as usual. She wiped tables, piled dishes, cleaned up broken crayons, explained the special of the day three dozen times, unclogged the toilet once, and brought food out to her last customer of the shift. But before she could lock the door, someone entered the diner.

There was always some jackass that decided to come in at 9:55 p.m. to order something right before they closed. She would never understand how someone could be so stupid. Whatever they ordered would be covered in spit—among other things she didn't want to think about.

She waited patiently for him to finish his meal and dropped subtle hints like, "Will that be all?" or "Would you like your check, sir?"

He finally walked out at ten-fuckin-thirty, and she made haste to clear his table. She had a hot date with ramen noodles, Netflix, and her pajamas. The thought of ripping off her bra almost sent her into pure ecstasy.

"I'm outta here," Eric called, heading to the door with his filthy apron slung over his shoulder.

"Really? You're just gonna leave me here all by myself?" she asked, trying to sound demure.

He snorted. "I've seen you kick the daylights out of every man who thought to grab you, remember?"

She smiled at the fond memories. "Yeah, yeah. Get outta here."

Not needing to be told twice, Eric turned and left.

She pulled out the mop, stacked the chairs, and got to work on the floor. Twenty minutes later, she was finally done and headed out to greet Ruby, her beat-up old car.

She patted the rust-bucket. "Hey, old girl. Miss me?" Ruby didn't reply, of course, that grumpy bitch.

It was a typical summer night, with cicadas aggressively screaming the songs of their people from the woods near the diner. She looked at the rest of the desolate parking lot and rooted around in her purse for her keys.

The hot air turned icy cold.

The owls stopped hooting.

The cicadas stopped screaming.

She stopped searching and looked around. Her breath was a cloud in front of her face. She couldn't see anything. She had perfect vision in the dark—a secret she didn't dare tell anyone. She had enough adjectives attached to her name. She didn't need "freak" added to the list. But this wasn't normal darkness. This darkness suffocated her as it closed in.

She was no longer alone; she could feel it. The prickling on the back of her neck. The way her arms broke out in gooseflesh. The slight shifting of the wind, bringing with it the smell of rancid rot. Her heart rate climbed at a rapid pace as fear set in. She still couldn't see anything, but the sensation of a nearby presence wouldn't go away.

A disembodied voice spoke into the empty air behind her. "Hello, my pretty. You look so delicious. I look forward to eating you."

She whipped around and still saw nothing. "You're going to eat me? How original. Did you look that up in Villain's for Dummies?" She spoke with all the bravado she could muster, but she could hear her voice wavering. "Show yourself, you slimy creep."

The disembodied laugh hit the air in front of her this time.

The sound was eerie and unnerving. She swallowed and stood her ground.

"You look just as delicious from this angle. I will eat those pretty little breasts first."

This thing was giving her the creeps. "Why don't you show yourself before you decide to eat me? I'd prefer to see my murderer." She reached back into her purse and wrapped her hand around her 9mm.

The voice let loose a guttural and sloppy sound akin to a laugh. "Be careful what you wish for, my delicious girl."

He appeared less than an inch in front of her, and his foul stench embraced her like a disgusting caress. She yelped and jumped back. She couldn't stop shaking at the sight of the living nightmare in front of her. He smiled, revealing a row of teeth sharp enough to cut through bones as if they were butter. His skin was the color of blood, and his beady, pitch-black eyes reminded her of beetles.

He grabbed her chin with his leathery hands, and a black claw sliced into her skin. "So soft. So smooth," he purred.

She screamed as his claw pierced her cheek, and warm blood ran down her neck. Her stomach lurched, making her gag. From his stench. From his touch. From his presence. The fucking gun was useless now. She couldn't stop shaking.

He continued to stroke her skin, leaving angry red lines that beaded with blood at each pass. His abnormally wide smile revealed each of his jagged teeth. "I don't know why the sky god wants you dead, and I don't care. With such soft skin and supple breasts, you will be quite delicious." He purred as his rough skin scraped over her neck.

The contact sent shivers down her body as fear engulfed her.

Come on, Mya. Get hold of yourself and fight him, she mentally pleaded.

She lifted her deadweight arm and struggled to control her breathing, coaxing her heart rate down. With a steadier hand, she gripped the gun and brought it up to the creature's disgusting chin.

She squeezed the trigger.

The sound assaulted her, making her ears buzz. She tried to cover them while shaking her head. The creature screamed into her face. He was pissed now. Her gun had done nothing. She watched as the bullet hole closed itself, even as the black goo blood dripped down the monster's face.

God, if you can hear me, I know I'm not much for prayer, but please don't let this thing eat me.

She'd reached a level of hysteria she'd never experienced before. She hated feeling useless. Long ago, she swore to herself she would never be a victim again, that she would always fight back. Her ex-boyfriend used her as a living punching bag, and it took her three years to get away from him. She ran as far as she could, bought a gun, and enrolled herself in martial arts classes—although she probably should've finished the classes. Now, here she was, all her efforts wasted. She was useless, defenseless, and weak. And she hated it.

The vile thing reached out to caress her chest, groping the flesh through her uniform. It jerked the blouse, and the buttons popped off. With its forked tongue, it licked the tender flesh above her bra line. She tried to reach up and push him away, but she found she couldn't move. The strap of her bra snapped apart, and the demon moved lower.

Do not throw up. Do not throw up, she chanted to herself.

Once the monstrosity found her nipple, he pulled it into his mouth and suckled it like a nursing newborn. He was fucking *playing* with her, and there was nothing she could do to stop him.

"So much beauty," he murmured against her breast, his hot breath making her gag and look away. "I can't wait to make you scream." He sank his jagged teeth into her sensitive breast.

White-hot pain shot daggers through her body.

Jesus Christ! She let out a cry before swallowing her scream. She wouldn't give him the satisfaction. Though, if he continued to devour his meal, she knew she would inevitably give in. She closed her eyes, trying to escape this hell.

Hot, sticky, black goo sprayed over her. She struggled to pry her eyes open and was awarded with a view of the creature's head as it rolled across the pavement. She stumbled backward, fell on her ass, and turned to retch until her stomach was empty. She raised her hand to wipe the trail of vomit from her lips and inadvertently smeared black goo into her mouth. With nothing left in her stomach, she began to dry heave.

She looked up and saw a man standing in front of her. He towered over her at well above six feet. He sported broad shoulders and a set of muscles that threatened to rip his shirt seams apart. His perfectly styled midnight-black hair seemed almost blue in the parking lot lights. The outfit he wore—fitted grey suit pants and a dress shirt—was at odds with the wicked, almost glowing sword he held. It dripped with black ichor.

She swallowed and pressed her diner uniform against the bloody wound on her chest. She was fairly sure she was missing some tit. She looked up into his ocean-blue eyes.

"Who the fuck are you?" she asked.

CHAPTER THREE

MYA

"Don't I at least get a thank you first?" he asked.

"Seriously?" she said with a scoff. "That . . . that *thing* just attacked me." She gasped as she put pressure on her chest wound to emphasize her point. "And it fucking hurt. But sure, thanks for saving me, I guess."

"You'll heal. It's not like he bit you anywhere else. I stopped him before that happened. You're welcome." He smirked.

She refrained from smacking the arrogant look off his face and lifted one brow. "Sure, he didn't eat the rest of my breast. Lucky me! But that doesn't mean it hurts any fucking less." Her voice had grown hysterical. *"Fuck!"* she yelled into the night sky.

A tissue fluttered in front of her to the ground. She looked at the man with contempt and ignored it.

"What was that thing?" she finally asked, staring at the creature's remains. It was still leaking black ooze everywhere.

"That is a demon," he said, leaning down to take a closer look at the head.

"I'm sorry. Excuse me one second." She turned around and screamed again. Composing herself, she faced the strange man once more. "A demon? Demons are real? You've got to be fucking kidding me." She walked over to the body and kicked it. "No fucking way."

"Yes, they're real," he said, standing and tugging on his tie to straighten it. "There is much we need to discuss, but not here. Come with me." He held his hand out to her as if she would take the hand of a crazy person who thinks demons exist.

"Right," she said, dragging out the word. She stared at him and crossed her arms defiantly, causing her to wince and bend over in pain. She uncrossed them with a huff.

He seemed to rethink his approach and advanced toward her as if she were a wounded, feral animal that might attack him. Which she was considering, to be fair. The only thing stopping her from shooting this psycho in the leg was that he had saved her from that monster. She shivered when she thought back to what that creature might've done to her.

"What's your name?" he asked.

"Mya," she muttered. "Yours?"

"Lir."

"Is that because of the way you look at people?"

"What?"

"Never mind. Why are you here? How'd you find me?" she asked. She had so many questions.

His blue eyes looked her up and down, lingering for a moment on her blood-soaked side. "You really don't know who you are?"

The question caught her off guard, and she stuttered before realizing she had nothing to say.

"Or why you were targeted?" he asked. Although, it felt a bit more like an interrogation than an inquiry.

"Nope. Why don't you tell me?"

He scrubbed his hand down his face in exasperation and looked up toward the sky. "Very funny." He returned his gaze to hers, spread his arms in a show of arrogance, and said, "Alright, here it is. I'm the leader of a small group of warriors called the Guardians of Terra. We were tasked with protecting you."

She stared back at him in disbelief. "Is this some kind of joke?" If so, she wasn't amused. She was exhausted, her boob ached, and she wanted to go home and pretend nothing happened.

What the fuck is a Guardian, and why do they need to protect me, of all people.

Though, she had asked for an adventure, hadn't she?

"Look, I don't have time for this 'joke' or whatever the fuck this is." She sucked in a breath. "What's wrong with you people?" Her voice sounded bold, considering she wasn't sure how much of her bravado remained.

He gestured to the dead demon. "Does that thing look like a joke to you?"

Well, no, she thought. It felt pretty real and had thoroughly scared the crap out of her. "Why did he want me?" she asked.

"You're a deity. A god—or goddess, if you prefer. As am I and the rest of the Guardians."

Oh my god. She almost snorted out a laugh. This wasn't real. This had to be someone's sick idea of a joke. There was no way she, a waitress at a diner, was a goddess. If she was some divine being, she wouldn't have needed help from this "knight in shining armor."

That's it!

Someone read her mind earlier and played this massive joke on her. That made much more sense than the whole god thing, right? Although, mind reading might be on the odd side as well. She'd been lost in thought for far too long and probably seemed like some sort of crazy person. She dared a glance back up at the towering god—lunatic? She hadn't yet decided.

He stared at her with utter disdain written on his face. He must have asked her a question or said something while she was lost in thought. "I don't have time for this shit," he said.

Some knight in shining armor he was. *More like Sir Anger Problems or Sir Impatience,* she thought, and laughed at her brilliant names.

He chanted something under his breath, and a portal opened up in the middle of the sky. He picked up the dead carcass with one hand and tossed it in, then grabbed the head and chucked that in, too. He chanted again, and the portal closed. He looked at her with a cocky grin.

"Do you believe me now?"

"Um, maybe?" she said.

"I guess I can work with that." He pulled out a cigarette, lit it, and let out a gentle moan as he inhaled the smoke. The sound of pleasure coupled with his deep voice was sexy.

Who was she kidding? All of him was sexy. If he had a personality transplant, maybe she'd try him out for a ride.

"I thought you said you were a Guardian. Don't Guardians protect people?" she asked.

"They do, and I am," he said on an exhalation of smoke.

"You know cigarettes kill people, too, don't you? Not to mention what they do to the environment?" She knew she was being petulant, but she was rattled and needed an outlet.

"Oh, please. Spare me your lecture, woman. I spend all my days working as a Guardian and ordering around a bunch of gods. You have no idea how stressful my job is. This is for me," he said, holding the cigarette like it was a lifeline.

"So why don't you use a vape instead?"

"What the hell is a vape?" He pinched the bridge of his nose. "Don't answer that. Just let me smoke in silence; this is supposed to be peaceful."

Alrighty then, she thought, and decided it was best for her personal safety to honor his request.

Five minutes and two cigarettes later, he spoke up. "Let's go. I'll take you to our safe house. It's where the other Guardians reside as well. We'll get you cleaned up and recovered, then we'll protect you while training you to use your powers."

She felt her pride rise to match his. "Wait just a minute. I don't even know you, and you certainly don't have the authority to tell me what to do. Is it too hard to just ask me politely?" She placed her hands on her waist and cocked her hip in silent challenge.

"If I had asked you politely, you would have said no. Then you would go to your own home and be dead by tomorrow." He shoved his hands into his suit pockets.

"Wow, thanks for that," she shot back.

"Please. Come. With. Me," he said, enunciating each word.

"What about my stuff? I at least need clothes and my car. I can't just leave it here."

"I'll send someone to grab your clothes and take your car back to your house."

She stared at him, contemplating his words. Did she dare go through that portal thingy with this sword-wielding stranger who sounded like a certified lunatic?

"Do you promise not to hurt me if I come with you?" she

asked. The question sounded perfectly reasonable to her—stranger danger and all that.

"Gods, what is *wrong* with you? If I wanted to kill you, why in the hell did I just save your life?" He shouted the questions at her.

"Chill, man." She pointed a finger at herself. "Remember? Traumatized?" She digested his words, and the demon flashed through her mind. "Good point. Fine, I'll come with you."

He lifted his sword and noticed the black ichor dripping from the blade. "Mother fucker," he muttered. He unceremoniously ripped off his shirt and used it to wipe his blade. Once he was finished, he swung it back into the sheath, leaving his torso bare.

She sucked in a breath as she studied the planes of his chest. His muscles appeared hard as granite. She longed to run a hand down them to test her theory. He definitely fought for a living. Her gaze scanned the various tattoos covering his upper body. They were intricate enough to almost distract from his rippling muscles. The archaic artistry was primordial in appearance. She recognized some as water symbols or sea creatures. It was hard to tell.

He caught her gawking and asked with a smirk, "Enjoying the view?"

"Yes," she replied shamelessly. She would not be embarrassed. The man was a literal god—and a shirtless one at that.

He shot her another smirk, opened a portal, and shoved her into it.

"Asshooooole," she screamed as the floor dropped beneath her.

And then she was spinning.

Falling.

CHAPTER FOUR

MYA

Falling still. Blackness. She closed her eyes and tried to ride it out. After an eternity—that was probably more like thirty seconds—her feet hit solid ground. Then her knees. Then she tumbled over and groaned in pain before she rolled and sat up.

An old, faded blue rug had padded her fall. The wooden floors beneath it appeared old as well, but well-cared for. No scuff marks or scratches in sight. A warm fire crackled merrily in the fireplace, and the cozy, overstuffed furniture set the tone for the rest of the room.

She could get used to this.

A massive, dirt-smeared hand appeared in front of her. The short nails were stained green. A smooth, masculine voice spoke from above. "Let me help you up."

She looked up to see yet another beautiful man, this one slightly taller than Lir and wider in stance. He had long white-blond hair, eyes the color of freshly mown grass, and a wicked smile that melted her ovaries. She grabbed onto his hand and let him help her to her feet.

"Nice to meet you. Name's Finn," he said.

"Mya," she murmured. She brought her outstretched arm back to her blood-soaked side, making sure to cover her exposed breast.

"What a beautiful name." He looked down at her disheveled state with a frown, a small measure of confusion clouding his features. "I see you were injured. We'll get you taken care of." He ushered her to the love seat by the fireplace.

"You're so much nicer than him." She nodded her head toward the jackass who brought her here.

"Ah, I see you already met our fearless leader, Lir." He winked at her and glanced at Lir. He then gestured across the room to a woman with silky, dark brown hair. She had hooded amber eyes and the kind of full lips that men went crazy for. "That beautiful woman over there is Jari."

Mya greeted her with a wave and a smile. "Hi, nice to meet you."

Jari beamed at her. "It's nice to finally have a woman in this testosterone nest. I'll get you some bandages and disinfectant to clean your wound."

Mya smiled at that. "Thanks for the help."

Jari nodded and left the room.

"Alex!" Finn shouted down the hall.

The largest man she'd yet seen appeared in the doorway. He wore a scowl and a blazing aura of confidence.

"Meet our guest. Her name's Mya." Finn pointed at her.

Alex grunted. "Nice to meet you," he said in a manner that didn't sound like he thought it was nice at all.

As she observed him, she wondered if he thought anything was nice. He was beautiful, too, but his beauty was sharp and almost cruel looking—dark brown hair, eyes that burned like fire under thick brows, a square jaw, and angry scars all over his body. She contemplated what it would take to give scars to a god and shuddered at the thought.

A massive tattoo of a dragon covered his right shoulder. The artwork was colorful and all too real, as if staring at the tattoo would cause it to morph into a living thing. He wore clothes that didn't belong in this century . . . there was a lot of leather.

Alex turned to Lir. "I thought she would be more . . . goddess-like. She looks like a child." He was as nice a guy as Lir appeared to be.

"She doesn't realize she's a goddess," Lir said.

Alex threw his arms in the air dramatically. "How are we supposed to train and protect a goddess who doesn't even know she's a goddess?"

Lir scrubbed a hand down his face in exasperation. He seemed to do that a lot around her. "I have no idea, but we need to work fast. We may need her for the war, and war is coming."

The leather-clad man scoffed and folded his arms over his chest. "I'm the god of war, Lir. You think I don't know when war is in the air?"

"Just telling it how it is," Lir said.

"Sweetheart, are you aware of any powers you may have?" Finn asked, his voice gentle.

Well, at least this guy is nice. "No, nothing out of the ordinary has ever happened to me. My life has been pretty boring until now," she said.

"You have any idea who your parents are, or what their powers are?" Finn prodded. He spoke with a slight, lilting accent.

"No, none. I grew up an orphan." Memories of the

multiple foster parents she'd grown up with popped into her mind. Always moving from one house to another, never able to make friends. Except one. She shoved that thought away. She'd long since given up being sad about her past.

Lir let out an irritated sigh and lit another cigarette.

Note to self: buy the guy some nicotine gum for Christmas.

"Great, we have *so* much information to go on. This is going to be fun," Alex said, voice as dry as the desert.

That statement infuriated her. Why must these gods treat her like this? She hadn't known she was a goddess. Part of her still thought this was some elaborate prank. "Look, I don't know what more you people want from me. Until an hour ago, I thought I was another boring, down-on-her-luck human like the rest of the population. Then this guy comes out of nowhere"—she waved her hand toward Lir—"and tells me I'm a *what?* A frickin' goddess! And you guys want me to give you answers?" She let out a humorless laugh.

This was ridiculous. She was so fed up with these gods. She was tired; everything in her body hurt from her brush with death and the trip through a fucking portal. She just wanted to take a nice, hot shower and climb into bed where she would hopefully sleep away this nightmare.

Jari came to the rescue with some first aid supplies, although the wound had stopped bleeding. She had always been a fast healer for some reason.

"Come on, we can work this out tomorrow," Jari said. "You need a hot shower, food, and some rest." Jari grabbed her arm and walked her to the stairs.

Mya let out a breath of relief. "Thank you. You're a lifesaver," she said as she winced up the stairs.

"I'm the one you should be calling a lifesaver!" Lir shouted from the living room.

26

So gods have exceptional hearing. Good to know. She would have to be quieter going forward.

"It's no problem at all. Happy to help," Jari said with a kind smile.

She escorted her up the stairs to a room on the right of the landing. It was just as cozy as the rest of the house. A blue comforter adorned the queen-size bed, reminding her how tired she was. A white dresser straight from a Pottery Barn catalog stood against a wall, with a chic mirror to match. An unlit fireplace and a moderately sized TV finished out the notable furnishings. She perked up at the television. She couldn't remember the last time she'd had one in her bedroom.

"Wait right here. I'll grab you some clothes," Jari told her.

She tested out the bed while she waited, easing onto the edge. It was every bit as comfortable as it appeared. She could have fallen right to sleep had it not been for the black goo still covering her. *I should probably get off the bed now.*

Jari returned with a stack of clothes and a towel. Handing over the bundle, she directed her to the modest bathroom off the main hallway. "I got you some Tylenol, too. You must be in pain." Jari smiled at her sympathetically.

"Tylenol works on the gods. Good to know." Mya grabbed the bottle a little too enthusiastically, but she was just so happy to have something to help with the pain. "Thank you so much. I officially love you."

Jari grinned. "You're welcome. I'll wait out here for a bit if you need me."

The bathroom door closed with a soft click. She took a moment to open the bottle of Tylenol and look around the bathroom. She found it to be quite clean, with double sinks and a shower/tub combo.

She swallowed the pills and got to the task of peeling off

her disgusting clothes. Her diner uniform had dried to her wound, and the gash reopened a bit as she peeled the top away from her skin. She looked down and inspected her injury.

Sharp, icy stabs of pain shot through her chest and down her arm. A small chunk of flesh seemed to be missing, but the most disgusting part was the black goo that oozed out of the injury. Mya gagged as she pressed her fingers along the edge of the wound. The black goo almost seemed to slither out of her. Yet another wave of nausea hit her as the sludge fell into the sink with a sickening thud.

Do not throw up, she silently pleaded with herself. She'd done plenty of that. She distracted herself by inspecting the skin instead.

Tiny marks from the thing's fangs surrounded what used to be a piece of her breast. She hoped it wouldn't look too deformed when the skin healed. She splashed it with the alcohol and swallowed down a scream, gritting her teeth against the sharp, stinging sensation.

Don't think about it.

After a few moments of teeth-grinding, scream-prompting pain, she slapped on a bandage and picked up her soiled clothes. They were definitely going in the trash. She hopped into the shower and let the hot water scald her skin. She watched the black goo slither down her body, nearly screaming as it appeared to come alive for a moment. The night's events tore into her mind with graphic clarity, and she shuddered.

No matter how much she washed, she couldn't get clean enough. She scrubbed at her skin until it was raw and red. She choked on a sob and tried to calm herself, but it was no use. It was so unfair. She'd worked so hard to get to this point.

The memories couldn't be stopped. The old men who got handsy and groped her—just like the demon, but much worse. Betrayal, abuse, and neglect. Her whole story had been dictated by others. When she was finally having a say, it had been ripped away again.

She jolted as she heard pounding on the door. "Yes?"

It was Lir. His voice was soft. "Just making sure you're okay. I thought I heard . . . crying."

"I'm fine. I'll be out in a minute," she said while trying to hide the obvious waver in her voice.

He hesitated. "Meet me in the kitchen, and I'll make you some food once you're out."

She was suspicious of his sudden kindness, but assumed it was pity. She hadn't expected that from the no-nonsense god. "Thanks."

"Alright then."

His footsteps grew faint as he walked away, and she let out the breath she'd been holding. She was alone again.

Thank god. Gods? Whatever.

She finished up her shower and toweled off. Her long black hair hung down her back in tangles, and her large brown eyes were swollen and red. She had a new cut across her jaw, but otherwise, she seemed the same. So why did she feel so different?

She inspected the clothes the goddess had given her, and she was pleased. Jari had brought her soft flannel pajama pants and a long-sleeved sweater. She eased into them, brushed her hair, and found she did feel better.

CHAPTER FIVE

JARI

J ari stepped outside the bathroom and leaned against the
hallway wall. She would wait for a few minutes, just to
make sure Mya was okay. It had been a long time since
she'd seen another woman in the Guardian's headquarters,
and she intended to protect her at all costs.

More importantly, she would be the absolute best friend
she could be because . . . well, she was lonely.

The guys were all right, but once you spent a few
centuries with the same three men, you ran out of things to
talk about. What do you say to someone who's been there for
every high and low point of your life? They did everything
together, and she would die for any of them without question,
but it was nice to have a woman to talk to.

She smiled as she remembered the last woman they'd had
in the Guardians—the fiery little goddess of sex, Aurora. Her
red hair had been perfectly wavy, as if she'd just come from
the beach. With big green eyes, a luscious mouth, and curves

that women longed to possess, she was every inch the sex symbol she was meant to be.

She thought back to one particular memory that always blazed brightest in her mind. The year was 1945, and the Guardians had been called to save some soldiers toward the end of World War II (the Guardians tried to save both sides of the War, as they were not supposed to discriminate). She and Aurora found themselves in an Army platoon and happened to walk in as the men were dressing. It was very pleasing to the eye. Men had evolved plenty over the centuries, but Jari always went weak in the knees for a military man.

Sharing that sentiment, Aurora convinced one soldier to orally pleasure another while she watched. Being the patron goddess of sex, she could feel the sexual tension between the men and encouraged them to act on it. An act that was vile and taboo back then. Thanks to Aurora, those men gained the freedom to embrace their forbidden homosexuality. She felt a little guilty that they were pressured into it, but it was too much fun! And they did end the night with an orgy that was enjoyable for all parties involved.

She didn't care that Aurora slept with all the Guardians, including herself. She wouldn't have passed up an opportunity to make love with the goddess of sex. It didn't matter that she was a woman. Jari spent centuries exploring her sexuality, and she wasn't afraid of a little adventure. She chuckled as she remembered when Lir had also slept with Aurora.

Gods, he'd acted so awkwardly afterward. As if we all thought he was a nun or some shit.

She wondered what Mya would think if she knew that tidbit. She'd caught the new little vixen staring at him once or twice already in the short time she'd been there. Each time, she would blush profusely. It was cute. *Now there's someone who's straight as an arrow,* she thought. *What stopped Mya from acting on her impulses? Is she still in shock?*

Jari sometimes forgot how long humans took to court each other. She viewed relations as a more casual endeavor. She had fallen in love once. The loss of her partner cut deep, and she never wanted to experience that feeling again. After that, she learned not to get too attached to a lover since they often died or grew apart—whether human or god.

The Guardians could have relationships with each other. There was no rule against it. Hell, she slept with Finn every few decades or so. He was fun to roll around with once in a while. Though she didn't dare fuck him any more than that for fear of a broken heart. That was the Finn specialty, and she didn't need to form an attachment any more than he did. Come to think of it, they were due for another rendezvous between the sheets, considering how much she was thinking about sex. Finn's room *was* just across the hall. Maybe she'd pay him a visit.

She chuckled. *Nah, too much work.*

❦

MYA

MYA HEADED DOWNSTAIRS toward the source of the quiet murmuring. She caught bits and pieces of the conversation.

"Who gave the order to rescue her?" someone said.

"Some general gave the order, but the tip was anonymous," Lir said. "Got there just in time, too. One of Beelzebub's demons was about to eat her for dinner."

Who was Beelzebub, and why did a demon want her? There had to be more to it than her status as a goddess. She didn't even have knowledge of her powers.

She caught Alex's gruff voice. "Do you think Zeus has aligned himself with the demons now?"

Zeus? She knew that one!

Lir spoke up again. "It's possible. He does have an unreasonable grudge against the human god."

She continued following the sounds of their voices and found them in the kitchen in the back of the house. It was square shaped with a small island, white cabinets, and grey quartz countertops. An old farmhouse-style table was tucked into the corner with six chairs around it. Jari and Alex were seated there, sharpening knives together.

How quaint.

Lir stood at the island, chopping vegetables. He was freshly showered, his black hair messy and damp. He wore a white t-shirt and gray sweatpants. She found him slightly more attractive than when he'd worn the duality of his suit and sword.

Finn strode in after her. "Ooh, the big bad boss man is making dinner," he teased. In one hand he held what appeared to be mushed up leaves and flowers. He stopped Mya with his clean hand. "Hold still," he ordered as he inspected the gash running down her cheek and jawline. He then smeared a generous amount of the earthy smelling goop on the wound.

She nearly sneezed.

"There. No scarring on that sweet face of yours," he said.

Lir picked up a bowl and a bag of salad, then tossed them to Finn. He fumbled but managed to catch it with his clean pinky finger and palm of his hand.

"Make the salad," Lir said without question in his voice.

Finn gave a pouty face. "Why me? My hands are dirty."

"You know good and well Alex and Jari can't do any of this shit without throwing some poison in." Lir pointed to the two in question.

Jari crossed her arms. "That was one time. *One!* And you didn't even die."

Finn paused from washing his hands. "I knew it! Do you know what I did to that poor toilet upstairs?"

Jari tossed her long, dark braid over her shoulder. "Yes. Lir made me clean it." She made a gagging face. "Remember?"

Finn, too busy apologizing to the lettuce, ignored her.

What a weirdo.

"We need to find out what type of goddess Mya is and get to work on releasing her powers," Jari said.

"Wait. I still think you guys have me confused with someone else. I'm not a goddess."

Jari whipped her head toward her. "You *are* a goddess. I can read the power levels of different beings, and yours definitely say goddess. Why else would the demon have been after you?" Jari shrugged as if she'd announced the weather instead of labeling Mya a goddess.

"You're telling me the demon thing attacked me because I'm a goddess?" Mya's voice held an air of skepticism.

Jari nodded. "You landed yourself in the middle of a war, and the god who hired that demon wants you dead."

"Dead? Why? If I am a goddess, I don't even have powers."

Finn stopped washing the lettuce. "That's what we're trying to find out. We need to know what powers you have, but more importantly, we need to know why Zeus wants you dead."

Mya sank into a chair as her legs gave out. "Zeus? Like the king of the Greek gods? Why would he want me dead?"

"We don't know," someone answered.

Mya was too busy freaking out to discern the owner of the voice.

Lir threw a piece of chicken into the sizzling pan. "You must be powerful for him to want you dead. Maybe you lost your memories, or your powers were bound. We're not sure, which is why we need to find a witch to help us."

"How do you propose we do that, genius?" Alex asked.

Finn answered him. "I should be able to. Witches are constantly using the earth for their rituals. Next time one of them does, I can find their location." He paused and stared into space for a moment. "In theory."

"Of course you want to find a witch," Alex said, disdain dripping from every word.

"We'll get to work on that tomorrow. For now, Mya needs to rest," Lir commanded.

She wasn't that surprised when no one voiced their complaint. He turned back to the stove and rotated the chicken around the pan.

She salivated, and her stomach grumbled. She hadn't realized how hungry she was. Fighting past the hunger, she noticed the salty scent of sea air wafting toward her from the open French doors.

"Where are we?" she asked.

"An island in Washington, close to Seattle. The boss likes being near the ocean," Jari said before she crunched down on a raw carrot.

Mya turned her attention to Lir. "So you're a god of the sea?"

"Figured that out all by yourself, did you?" he shot her an annoyed look.

She ignored him and turned to Jari. "What are you a goddess of?"

"I'm a goddess of snakes, poisons, secrets . . ." she waved her hand as if it meant to go on.

Cool, she thought. *Alex is a god of war, so that leaves*

35

Finn. She turned to him and opened her mouth, but he was already answering her.

"I'm the god of plant life," he said. He lifted his palm. She watched in amazement as his skin turned green, and a flower sprouted out of his finger.

She pulled out a chair from the table and sat down. "Are you all Greek gods like Zeus? I don't know much about Greek mythology . . . or any mythology, really. There's a lot of gods that I don't know about. I'm kinda just scraping together what I learned in high school."

Jari picked up the knife she was sharpening and tossed it around in the air, making Mya flinch a bit. Her movements were quick, and she handled the weapon in a way Mya had never seen.

"We're not all Greek gods," Jari said. "Though most of the gods alive today are from the Greek pantheon. I'm a Maori goddess. I was once called Ngarara, The Divine Serpent. Alex is Greek, Lir is Irish, and Finn doesn't really know, but he spent many centuries in Ireland. That's how he and Lir met."

Mya considered how varied their ethnic backgrounds and domains were. gods of the sea, snakes, war, and plants, all saving people together. One merry band of misfits.

"How did you all end up as Guardians?" she asked.

Lir slid a plate of food in front of her, his blue eyes as intense as the scowl painted on his face. "That's a story for another day. Eat your food."

Jeez, the man is so damn bossy.

While everyone ate their food in silence, she ravaged it, chewing loudly. She devoured her entire plate in mere minutes. She leaned back and patted her full stomach, the fatigue finally setting in. She was ready for bed now.

Finn stood, stretching his bulky body. "I'm off to bed!"

He walked to Mya and brushed a lingering kiss on her temple. "If you need anything at all, my bedroom is just across the hall from yours." He took another step and stopped, smirking as he looked back at her. "Fair warning . . . I sleep in the nude." His tone was playful as he shot her another one of his panty-melting smiles.

She would have been flattered, except something told her Finn was a lover of all women.

"Understood! Thanks, Finn," she said, and couldn't help but smile back.

He winked and left the room. Jari flashed her a knowing smile—the woman could definitely read minds.

Lir glared at her and stood from his chair. "I'm off to bed, too." He turned to the two remaining gods. "You guys are on kitchen duty." He left the room, taking the lively atmosphere with him. The room felt empty without his overwhelming presence. At the very least, he was nice to look at.

With that last thought, Mya ventured to her cozy little room at the top of the stairs and fell asleep.

❧❦❧

SHE WOKE TO the brutal sun glaring into her eyes. *Ugh, I thought Washington was supposed to be cloudy.* She already hated waking up in the morning, and now the damn sun wouldn't leave her alone. To top it all off, someone was pounding on her door.

Jari entered the room with a wide smile, her dark hair tied back in a ponytail. "Rise and shine, buttercup! Sun's up, get your butt up!" She sounded like someone's mother, and Mya hated her more for it.

She half-mumbled, half-yelled, "Go away!"

"No can do," she said in a chipper voice. "The boss likes to get to work bright and early."

Of course he did.

"The boss can kiss my *ass!*" she shouted.

"I wouldn't say that to him if I were you," Jari said with a chuckle.

She listened for more, but it appeared Jari's morning assault was finished. She rolled onto her stomach and pulled her pillow over her head. Maybe now Jari and the sun would finally leave her alone.

Seconds later, her door exploded open. She was shocked it didn't fly off the hinges with the force. Lir stood before her in all his suited perfection, his large body blocking the doorway.

Meanwhile, she probably had a bad case of bed head and morning breath.

He took long strides to the bed and scooped her up as if she weighed nothing. He set her on her feet. "Get up, day's wasting."

God, I hate this meddling bastard. Why couldn't he just let her sleep? She'd had an eventful night and was still in need of some recovery. "What is wrong with you? I'm not a two-year-old. Let me sleep, you jerk," she pouted, sounding exactly like a two-year-old.

She mumbled some curse words about what he could do with his breakfast and set to work getting ready.

CHAPTER SIX

FINN

F inn woke to the sound of moaning. His dick jacked up to attention. Excited, he turned to the source of the moan. *Wait.* It was his stupid alarm clock. He'd fallen for it again. Jari had gifted him the alarm clock for Christmas years ago, funny girl. That damn thing got him every morning.

He swung his legs over the bed and went to his closet to get dressed.

What to wear, what to wear. He browsed his shirts and found some suitable candidates for the day. He pulled out his Guardians of Assholes shirt—always a good one. Or he could wear his Jingle Balls shirt with a big picture of hairy balls printed across the front. He loved saving people while wearing that one. Another shirt caught his eye, and he pulled it out. It was his Lir Sucks Dick shirt.

Perfect! He did a smell check. *Not bad.*

He was just gonna get dirty while rolling around in the grass, anyway. He pulled his blond hair into a pony, not bothering with a brush.

He headed downstairs to get himself the Finn breakfast specialty: a beer. He found Lir in the kitchen, already cooking. He was decked out in his typical suit. Today it was an expensive-looking grey jacket and pants paired with a black shirt and a tie. He couldn't understand why Lir insisted on wearing suits, or how he could even manage to fight in them. Finn was a t-shirt and jeans man himself. He especially loved his motorcycle boots. They were excellent for crushing skulls.

Lir turned toward him and frowned. "I thought I told you to burn that shirt," he said.

"Now, why would I get rid of something that irritates you to no end?" he asked.

"I'll burn it myself, then," Lir said.

"I'll buy another."

"Child."

"I know you are, but what am I?" Finn sang.

Lir scrubbed his hand down his face and ripped a cigarette from his pocket. "Irritating bastard," he muttered.

Finn grinned at him and snatched a piece of bacon from the pan. "Right, then. I'll leave you alone. I'll just be outside, rolling around on the ground, singing to the animals, trees, and shit," he said. With that, he stepped outside to begin his task of finding a witch, whistling a merry tune on his way out the door, just to annoy Lir.

Annoying Lir was one of his favorite activities.

He strolled through the green grass. The wind stirred his hair as the salty sea air tapped into his senses. He walked over to his beloved place beneath the apple tree. The tree's strong roots always helped ground him. This was his happy place— his peace and serenity. He would gladly stay out there all day if he could, lying under the shade of the tree and being one with the plants surrounding him.

The truth was, he always held on to the belief that he was born directly from the earth itself. He didn't have a childhood, or if he did, he didn't remember one. Finn only remembered being an adult and didn't recall any parents.

Some gods had suggested he came from Gaia herself, but Finn wouldn't accept that because if she were his mother, that meant she had abandoned him—an idea he refused to consider. He struggled through his thoughts, trying to find those old memories. It had been so long ago. Finn didn't even know how old he was. He just remembered when the humans came to be. He remembered watching the repulsive little creatures as they changed, constantly and rapidly.

The humans disgusted him with the way they treated their environment, littering and destroying all the wonderful things nature gave them with their incessant thirst for more. Finn slapped a cap on those feelings. He had to. He was a protector for the humans, and no matter what he thought of them, he still had hope they would redeem themselves.

He kneeled on the ground and shoved his hands into the depths of the rich soil. A flood of power surged through him as the earth fed him its strength. His hands and eyes glowed green. In return, the flowers, trees, and even the weeds started gravitating toward him. He let the flower vines crawl up his body, wrapping around his limbs. He didn't mind. He knew the plants wouldn't harm him. They recognized his strength and pushed against him, the thorns biting into his skin, asking for his power. To appease them, he gave a little of what he had. Once they were sated, the vines released him, traveling back to their proper places.

He then began chanting in old Gaelic, asking the trees and the earth to find the power he sought—to find those who worshiped the sacred ground.

The earth answered his call and showed him the way. The

ground pulsated beneath him. He zeroed in on the energy and tracked a witch to her location. *Got you!* he thought proudly. *I'm still a god, bitches.*

He rinsed the dirt away with a garden hose and headed to the house to share his news.

⚫⚫⚫

MYA

MYA WALKED INTO the kitchen, inhaling the scent of bacon. It made her mouth water and her stomach growl. The thought of shoving a few strips into her mouth almost made up for the rude wake-up call. Lir stood at the stove, flipping the bacon, an apron tied around his crisp black dress shirt. She was a little shocked that he was cooking again. She assumed by his attitude thus far that he would implement the "taking of turns" and "fair is fair" type duties, complete with a color-coded chore chart.

Maybe he just likes to cook?

She could live with that.

Jari was seated at the table again, but she was chopping potatoes with an actual sword this time. *Logical.* Her voluminous hair trailed over her shoulder in a braid, her longsword strapped to her back. She wore a black leather jacket over it, and she looked so badass, Mya felt a pang of jealousy. Ignoring her feelings, she chose kindness.

"Where are Finn and Alex?" she asked.

"Finn is outside connecting with the earth and finding us a witch. Alex is sleeping," Jari said.

"Why does he get to sleep while I get dragged out of bed?" She pointed her question at Lir, making sure he got a full view of her scowl.

The bastard had the audacity to smile at her. "Your angry face is adorable. Kind of like a little kitten about to pounce," he teased.

"Answer the damn question," she snarled.

He assessed her tone and decided to answer her. "When you see Alex fight, you'll understand."

"Oh, so because I'm a weak little female, I don't get the same privileges?" She crossed her arms.

He gave her an unamused stare. "Don't pull that feminist crap with me! It has nothing to do with you being female. When I need Alex, I drag his ass out of bed too. It just so happens we don't need him for this activity."

She knew she was being unreasonable and calmed down a little. Although, something told her Lir's answer wasn't the real reason he let Alex sleep in. She would just have to make sure to be there for that wake-up call. She would love to see Alex beat Lir into the ground.

"I guess that's fair," she said.

"Of course it is," he said.

Ugh, this guy.

Finn burst into the kitchen; his eyes were bright and wide with excitement. He resembled a five-year-old headed to the candy store. "Let's go witch huntin', boys and girls!"

Jari jumped up from her task, knocking the potatoes onto the floor. "Yes! I am so effing bored! Let's go!"

"Now, wait just a minute." Lir gestured for them to sit down. "We need to eat first. Jari, now you have to redo the potatoes."

She looked down at the ground. "Oops. Five-second rule?"

Lir raised an eyebrow. She sighed and got to work cleaning up her mess.

❦

MYA LANDED on her side on the stained and dirty sidewalk and promptly cast up her breakfast. *I have to get used to traveling by portal.* She was tired of falling and didn't want to throw up ever again. Twice in two days was plenty, thank you.

"Where are we?" she asked.

"Somewhere in St. Louis," Lir said.

She looked up at the old, red brick building.

"The witch is upstairs, apartment 3B," Finn told them.

They climbed the rickety metal staircase and hunted down the apartment. Lir pounded on the door like a police officer looking for a suspect.

She's so not going to answer now.

He pounded on the door again. "It's the Guardians of Terra. We need to speak with you immediately. Open the door!" Authority saturated his every word.

They waited again, and still no one answered. With unsettling ease, Lir kicked the door in. A heavy metallic scent hung in the air, greeting them as they entered. Something was definitely wrong in this apartment. They took a few steps in and found a dead witch.

They had just walked into a crime scene.

CHAPTER SEVEN

MYA

Mya followed the rest of the Guardians inside with caution. The hallway leading to the interior of the apartment was tinted red with blood, and the wet carpet squished beneath her feet.

She avoided the urge to look down and find out why.

Broken bits of wood from the obliterated furniture littered the floor. A television with a smashed screen stood beside an upended couch. The more she looked around, the more appalled she became at the amount of blood covering every surface. *How could one body hold so much blood?*

After what felt like a century, they found the witch. Well, they found the witch's body. Half of her body . . . pieces.

Mya's stomach heaved as nausea crept up.

Oh my god, don't throw up again, you wimp, she chided herself.

Bite marks covered the mangled body, as if something had eaten her. The stomach and organs were gone, as were her breasts. To her horror, she scanned up the body and found two hollowed-out areas where the witch's eyes used to be. Mya wondered if it was the same type of demon that attacked her.

Do not throw up! She swallowed back the bile. *That was disgusting. Should've just thrown up; they already think you're weak.*

She forced her gaze away from the scene and pulled herself back to the present conversation.

"This was the same type of demon that attacked Mya. There's a target on her back now, no doubt," Lir said.

"No shit, Captain Obvious," Jari bit out.

Lir shrugged. "We need to get out of here before the cops arrive."

As they turned to leave, the witch's head lurched upward and levitated a few feet above the floor. Blood dripped from the gaping hole in her detached neck. Mya let out a startled scream. The witch opened her mouth, and Mya struggled to hold in another scream as fear riddled her. The dead, eyeless head was now *speaking!*

> *"The night shall be found*
> *A crown of laurels will adorn Death*
> *Poison will dance upon the ashes*
> *The one god will fall"*

The witch choked out a black mist, and her head dropped to the floor, once again lifeless. It thudded against the sticky carpet.

"What did any of that mean?" Mya looked over at her comrades for guidance.

They appeared just as mystified as she was, their faces drained and pale. It was comforting to know she wasn't alone in her confusion and fear. It was also frightening. Weren't these people gods? Shouldn't they know about this kind of thing?

A guttural laugh echoed in the tiny apartment. The sound reminded her all too well of her own brush with a demon. Another laugh followed, indicating there was more than one demon this time. She whipped her head toward the source of the voice, wishing she had a weapon.

Black goo splashed onto her face as the demon appeared, sprawled across the ground. Finn stood above it, holding a goo covered axe. She hadn't even seen him move.

How the fuck did he do that?

A lamp crashed into her before she had time to dodge. She recovered quickly, swiping glass out of her hair. She spotted Jari flying through the air, kicking one of the monsters. She tried counting the blurred shapes but lost track.

Jari landed a spinning back kick, elbowed another, and then swung her blade into the gut of a third. Without pause, she whipped around and sliced the head from one more. Her maneuvers were fluid. They fell into place, one after another, like it was all the continuation of a single, long movement. She didn't falter—not once—and she was glorious in her brutal dance.

At the beginning of her final act, she sling-shotted a demon into two others and swung her blade into both their necks with one well-placed stab. Their black blood sprayed everywhere as their heads rolled away. She circled around, landing blows on the remaining demon before her last blow relieved him of his head as well. The whole thing took about six seconds, and every single demon was dead.

Jari straightened, chest heaving with victory. She wiped her dual blades against the already dirty couch.

A childish whine from Finn pulled Mya's attention away

from Jari. "Hey! You only let me kill one demon. That's so not cool."

"Next time, move faster," Jari teased back.

Finn shot her his typical wicked smile.

"Where was Lir?" Mya asked. She looked around and found him leaning against the wall, smoking a cigarette. Not a single hair on his head was rumpled. *Did he even fight?*

"Thanks for your help," Jari said to him dryly.

"You didn't need my help. There were only a few of them," he said with a wave of his hand.

Jari shrugged her agreement. "True."

"Plus, you were just saying you were bored this morning. Maybe you'll stop complaining now." Lir was being a snot.

Finn snorted. "Debatable."

Lir put out his cigarette on the wall and, on his exhalation of smoke, he said, "Okay, time to leave." He opened another portal.

Exactly what she needed—to travel in a portal again.

❦

SHE FELL INTO THE BLACK, spinning tunnel and braced herself. She would not fall and look like a fool again. The floor of the safe house living room rushed toward her all too fast.

Wait, I can see the floor this time. This is good. I can do this. She bent her knees and landed with a thud. She rocked a bit, still dizzy, but she managed to stay upright.

"Yes!" she shouted to the room.

The Guardians looked at her like she had suddenly grown three heads.

"Sorry, I got a little excited there. I finally landed without falling on my ass!" she said, laughing to herself.

48

The Guardians were still unimpressed. They probably always landed on their feet, like the over-accomplished lot they were.

"We need to find out what that prophecy meant," Jari said, changing the topic.

Lir nodded. "Agreed."

"We need another witch. I'll get to work finding one," Finn said. He took off down the hallway, skidding to a stop when he heard a booming voice behind him.

"No!" Lir said, his voice loud and firm. "I don't want another witch dead because of us. We find one the old-fashioned way. Research."

Jari stomped her foot and whined. "Ugh. Research is so boring."

"We've no other option." Finn shook his blond head, his voice just as whiny.

Lir led them into what looked like a library. Tall wooden bookshelves lined the hunter-green walls, and a small desk sat in the corner. There was yet another fireplace—the house seemed to be full of them. Leather couches and armchairs surrounded it. But Mya's eye was drawn to a Harry Potter rug in the middle of the room.

"Who's the Harry Potter fan?" she asked with too much excitement in her voice.

"That would be me," Finn said proudly.

"What's your house?" She was secretly ready to judge him as a person based on his response.

"Gryffindor. Duh. I'm a Guardian," he said, as if there were no other options.

"I'm a Guardian, too, and my house is definitely Slytherin," Jari announced. This made sense. She was a goddess of snakes, after all.

49

"The boss pretends he doesn't care, but he likes Harry Potter too," Finn whispered to her.

"I heard that, and my house is Ravenclaw," Lir said, all matter-of-fact.

Finally, something in common. Though she didn't dare tell him that.

Lir pulled down books and tossed them to the group. "We need to read about coven rituals and holidays. Find out when the nearest congregation is happening." He continued stating objectives. "I want anything and everything you can find on prophecies too. We need any info you can dig up on local witches, their names, families, practices, allies. There should be a book around here somewhere that lists all the local family trees." He continued searching for all the books they would need.

Mya picked up one of the books with a sigh. "Can't we just Google this stuff?"

Lir's wide blue eyes stared at her. "Google? What is Google?"

Everyone laughed at Lir's absurd question.

He folded his arms across his chest, his massive biceps bulging against his shirt seams. The entire room quieted down.

"You really don't know what Google is?" Mya asked in a hushed whisper.

"Obviously."

"It's a search engine, and very useful. Don't you have internet service in this house or on your phones?"

Finn pulled his phone out of his pocket. "There's internet on this thing?"

"Yes. How are you guys not current on your under-standing of technology?" Mya asked with a laugh.

Jari snapped her head up to stare at Mya with her eerie

snake eyes. "Some of the gods tend to hide for years, some of them live in another realm, and some choose to stay away from humans at times."

Finn shrugged. "I like to be closer to nature, and technology is far from natural."

Mya glanced at Lir, but he was turned away from them. She sighed. "So why can't I use the internet at least? I actually understand it."

Jari bit her plump lip. "We can't use the internet because our enemies could be watching us. Unfortunately, we have to research the old-fashioned way—with books."

At least one of them knew what the internet was and why they couldn't use it.

"I'll go make some coffee," Mya said, resigned to her fate of spending the day holed up in the library.

No one responded. The room could've been empty for all they were paying attention to her. She made her way to the kitchen.

CHAPTER EIGHT

MYA

Mya looked up from the tenth book she'd read that evening. She rubbed her aching temples and snatched her coffee cup from the table.

Empty? Again? She'd already used up the last bit of coffee grounds she found in the dark corners of the kitchen. It tasted as disgusting as it looked, but she choked it down anyway. How many hours had she been holed up in here? She looked at the books littering the coffee table. They now had various page markers throughout them.

She tried to sift through her brain and make sense of it all. Looking around to see what the other gods discovered, she noticed Jari reclined in a chair, asleep.

Bitch.

Finn tossed a ball in the air and caught it while simultaneously eating a snack. Lir was nowhere to be found.

Typical.

He just gave the orders. He wouldn't dare occupy himself with such a mundane task as research.

She rooted around for a notebook and started writing down the information they needed, desperate to organize her thoughts. *The nearest Coven ritual was . . . ?* She looked around to find the right book. Once found, she opened it and scanned the pages until she discovered what she was looking for. *Got it! Litha!* The summer solstice ritual was in two months. She reached for the book filled with family trees, open right where she left it on the floor.

She studied the picture for a moment. The local coven was quite large and filled with only women, every one of them beautiful, willowy, and blond. They had the typical American family name of Anderson. She wrote that down. *Next? The prophecy? Yes, that's it.* She looked around, closing books as she went.

Her head threatened to split open. She needed to take a break, and now that she thought about it, her stomach growled in anger for food. When was the last time she'd eaten?

"Aren't you done yet?" Alex asked her, his voice amused.

How long had he been watching her? She glared up at him from her seated position on the rug.

"Well, hello, sleeping beauty. Did you enjoy your beauty rest?" She smirked.

He leaned back, planted two large boots on the coffee table, and rested his muscular arms behind his head. She tried not to stare or drool. Wanting to jump into bed with one asshole deity was more than enough for her.

He grinned broadly. "Yes, I did. Did you enjoy your morning of research?" he asked with an undertone of laughter.

"Oh yes, it was very enjoyable indeed."

"Come on, I can hear your stomach growling from here. Let's get some lunch. My treat."

"Your treat? Can we go anywhere I want?" She grinned while scrambling to her feet.

"Anywhere reasonably affordable." He dropped his boots to the ground with a thud and swung his body up. "Come on, let's go!" He bent over the coffee table, picked up a book, and threw it across the room at a still sleeping Jari. It landed solidly on her lap with a resounding thud.

She screamed awake. "What the hell?"

"Come on, books don't hurt you. And sleeping on guard duty? Shame." He shook his head at her, waggling a finger.

She scowled and chucked the book back at him. Alex whipped his body to the side. The book flew past him, crashed into the wall, and fell to the floor.

Lir walked into the room, wearing a pair of gym shorts and a tank instead of his normal suit. Mya took her time, admiring his physique.

"We got an SOS call. Let's go. Gear up!" His words effectively killed the jovial mood in the room.

Jari wiped the drool off her chin and jumped up from her chair.

"What about me?" Mya asked.

"I want you to stay here, where it's safe. We'll be back as soon as we can," Lir commanded.

"But I can help."

"Mya, you're a liability right now, and we need to protect you," he said firmly.

A part of her knew he was right. Plus, she could use this time to really explore the house. If a leg of her tour involved his room, that would be okay with her.

And, per Lir, she would remain safe and sound.

LIR

Lir reread the SOS call with trepidation. A group of sailors off the coast of Italy sent the call through their radio to the local coast guard. Once they mentioned the nature of the call, it was rerouted to Lir.

Normally, Lir wouldn't be the least bit worried, but the sailors reported sightings of giants with one eye. That could only be the cyclopes. The vicious, one-eyed creatures were a part of Zeus's army. What if Zeus was there? While Lir was powerful, he was unsure if he could battle with the great and mighty one. Even if all the Guardians helped him, they might still lose. Leaving the humans to their fate crossed his mind, but he quickly pushed it away. No, that wouldn't do. He might have been a deity, but he still had what the humans ironically called "humanity."

He could contact Death. Lir was the only Guardian with the authority to call upon him, but they never knew what mood he would be in. He would save that for the ultimate "Hail Mary." He would just prepare for battle, use the sea to aid him, and hope for the best outcome.

Lir changed into his battle gear, strapped a sword to his back, and sheathed his backup blades to his thighs. He grabbed his bow and some throwing stars as well. With adrenaline coursing through his veins, he led the Guardians into another potential death trap to save the humans. Anticipation filled him.

This was what made being a Guardian worthwhile. Not the paperwork or the political bullshit. Simple, good old-fashioned fighting. And saving people, of course. He jumped into a portal, the other Guardians following on his heels.

The screams of wounded men greeted them. The ship was sinking; only half of it lay tilted above the water. The cyclopes hurled rocks, debris and all manner of things from another ship a few hundred meters away. As Lir surveyed the scene, an unfortunate man lost his grip and fell into the water, screaming. With a sickening slap, he sank into the choppy sea, and an uncomfortable silence followed. Lir felt a stab of pain in his heart. It was too late to save him.

He let loose a bellowing scream and called the sea to him. His mind probed the deep waters, searching until he found an ally in the great expanse. He called the nearby whale to him. The massive beast latched on to the connection and swam toward the fight. The whale responded with a mighty heave, restoring the foundered ship to its proper position.

Dead bodies rose with the wreckage. Their blood mixed with the seawater, giving it a rusty tinge. Lir's rage welled up, and he shouted a command to the cyclopes, demanding they stop their onslaught before he ended their pathetic lives. He knew they wouldn't comply. Admittedly, a part of him banked on their brutality.

Calling the sea to him once more, he let the waves carry him to the other ship. He unsheathed his sword, cracked his neck, and readied his stance. Heads were about to roll. He landed firmly on the ship and allowed the water to continue dancing around him in swirls of beautiful menace. He was stronger for it.

One of the monsters turned in his direction and threw a boulder. *Pathetic.* Lir effortlessly batted it away with a stream of water. With that same jet, he enveloped the creature's head, watching as it struggled to breathe. Knowing the cyclops was as good as dead, he turned his attention to the rest of the battle.

Alex shot an arrow into a cyclops's eye while simultaneously kicking another and stabbing it in the thigh. The second cyclops bellowed and fell onto his knees.

Mine, Lir thought.

He raced toward the monster, held his longsword out, and swung. The head remained in place for just a moment before sliding clean off.

No, this is too easy, Lir assessed. He would never release his frustration this way.

Jari and Finn stood on the other ship battling another cyclops as Alex finished off the one he'd shot in the eye.

Lir looked around and found no other monsters. Frustrated, he screamed into the open ocean air. "Zeus, where are you, you bastard? I know it was you. You can stop hiding from us." He waited and was rewarded with nothing.

Rage engulfed him. He was angry with Zeus for sending the cyclopes. Angry he could not save the sailors—the men who still believed in him! He was beyond furious, and he began to rip the ship apart in a frenzied rage.

Water swirling around him, he sensed the sea roiling up in indignation to appease him. The waves splashed into him. He was so caught up in the writhing chaos, he was surprised to find he was standing in water with nothing left to destroy. He used the sea to propel himself back onto the other ship where the Guardians waited.

He landed on the deck with a wave of water following him. The ship groaned in protest, but held strong. He looked up at the sky again and screamed himself hoarse. "Zeus, we will meet, and I will destroy you! These humans did not deserve to die today! Mark my words, you will perish!" He finished on the threat, knowing the cowardly god king wouldn't respond.

A comforting hand rested on his shoulder. It was Finn, offering his support. "Lir, there's nothing more for you here. Why don't you go home and check on Mya? We'll stay and clean up this mess."

It was probably best for everyone if he agreed and left at this point. He released some of his simmering anger with great effort. "Alright, see you at home."

When he arrived at the safe house, he checked on Mya first and found her asleep in the library. He left her alone; she needed the rest. He decided he would go for a swim in the sea to release his tension. He entered his room and was greeted with a surprise. A busty little blond waited in his bed . . . and she was naked.

Katie. Shit. He forgot he made plans with her. Worse yet, he kept forgetting to break up with her. He knew it was wrong. They'd been sort of dating for a few months now. There was nothing wrong with her, but he knew the longer he put off the inevitable, the more his actions would hurt her. She really was a sweet girl—not to mention a true bombshell —and she didn't deserve that kind of pain. That was always the problem, though. She was sweet, and he . . . he was not.

She ran a hand down her trim stomach until it landed at the juncture between her thighs. His dick woke up, and he decided he'd break up with her tomorrow.

Yep, definitely tomorrow.

"Hey, baby," she pouted. "I waited hours for you."

That was all it took to snap him out of his hazy desire and lose his hard-on.

"I'm sorry," he said flatly. "My job kept me busy. Let me clean up. I'll be right back." He headed into his bathroom and stripped off his bloody clothes. He studied his reflection in the mirror. "You're an asshole," he said to himself.

CHAPTER NINE

MYA

Mya woke with a jolt. *No, no, no,* she thought. She had planned on snooping and ended up wasting all her alone time sleeping. She peeled her face off the book she'd been reading before she crashed from boredom. She stretched and then paused, listening for any signs that she was no longer alone.

Silence.

The Guardians must still be out on their "mission" or whatever. There was time; she would just need to hurry.

She ran upstairs to scout the rooms and found Finn's first. It reeked of stale beer and . . . sex? *Gross. He could at least buy an air freshener or maybe light a candle. Jeez.* She stepped over a banana peel and rooted around in his closet. Finding nothing of interest, she headed to his dresser. It was comprised of underwear, porn, more porn, sex toys, and condoms. *Jesus.* This was useless. She wouldn't find anything in Finn's "red room."

She entered the room adjacent to his and discovered what

she guessed was Jari's room. It was comically different from Finn's. Her room was so neat, Mya hesitated to search it for fear Jari would know immediately. She backed up and exited.

She found Alex's room at the end of the hallway. That meant Lir's room was downstairs. She'd take a quick peek here and head down to explore the room she was really interested in.

Alex's room didn't look like it belonged to the god of war, but then none of their rooms looked like the deities currently residing in them. Crimson sheets donned the unmade king-size bed. A mini fridge sat beside it and doubled as a nightstand. She checked his closet and found racks and racks of weapons: knives, swords, an ax, and even guns. *Is that a flamethrower? Awesome!* She would have to convince him to let her use it one day. She moved on to his dresser and found nothing but clothes. *No porn? How boring.* She was curious to find out if he was a BDSM man.

With nothing else to look for, she headed downstairs and found Lir's room.

As she reached for the handle, a low, womanly moan drifted toward her from behind the door. Her heart raced, and her pulse pounded in her ears as she started to tiptoe backward. The door swung open.

Shit on a cracker! Oh my god, he's naked! Well, damn near it!

She tried to look unaffected by his god-like body.

He draped his arm on his door frame and spoke in a husky tone that nearly melted her. "Do you need something?"

"Who, me? Uh, no? Um, sorry," she choked out, aware she sounded like an absolute idiot.

She spotted the beautiful blond on the bed, totally naked and unashamed. She had the kind of body one could only get through daily workouts and eating nothing but salad and air.

Mya momentarily imagined stabbing her with one of Alex's knives.

He wouldn't notice just one of them missing.

She had no reason to be jealous. Lir certainly wasn't hers. She discreetly wiped her mouth.

At least there was no drool.

He looked at her with a smirk and asked, "So, you don't need anything, and you just happened to be standing outside my door. Is that it?"

She couldn't think of a good response, so she tried to turn the tables. "I didn't knock. How'd you know I was standing here?" She cocked a hip and gave him her best stern look.

He chuckled. "Because when you move, you sound like a baby rhino."

Rude.

"It's really nothing. I was just, uh, checking if you guys were back yet, and you are . . . so bye." She turned and left before her face turned a deeper shade of crimson. The heat burned on her cheeks.

God, that was embarrassing.

CHAPTER TEN

ALEX

Seagulls squawked as they fought over a piece of flesh from the dead sailors on the broken ship deck.

Alex had spent the last hour collecting wallets for identification. He'd learned over the centuries that although the lives were lost, the families needed closure to grieve and move on. Otherwise, they'd have false hope that their husband, brother, sister, or friend was just "lost at sea" and would find their way home. There was no hope for these poor souls.

He looked around for Finn and saw him speaking with the local police. Damn cops had been grilling them for the last hour with every question imaginable like, "Did you know these men?" He snorted and imagined saying, "Why yes, officer, I did, and I came all the way out here to another country, just to kill them. Then I called you, because that's what murderers do, right?"

If that wasn't irritating enough, crime scene experts were walking all over the place, bumping into him, and crowding his space. He would've just left and told Lir he did what he could, but the fucking cops wouldn't let him leave.

He kicked at a body. "Thanks for ruining my night," he muttered and shook his head. "Humans are so weak."

Why the hell did I become a Guardian, anyway?

He liked to fight, sure, but the unappreciated task of saving the ungrateful little humans grew tiresome. The puny beings didn't even believe in the gods, let alone the Guardians. Yet the Guardians saved them time and time again, and for what? There was no gratitude. No belief.

He remembered when the humans knew him as Ares, and the battles had been glorious. He was no longer Ares; that god disappeared when the humans no longer made an offering or asked for his favor. He chose to reinvent himself. Alexander to most, and Alex to those he cared about.

"Alex!" Jari called, snapping him out of his thoughts.

A thick fog swirled in the air. The cops were nowhere to be found.

What sort of Stephen King shit is this?

A womanly figure appeared out of the mist. She was striking, and as he suspected, she wasn't a human at all. It was Hecate, the goddess of magic. He'd thought she was long dead and was somewhat shocked to see her. Magic had been the first thing the humans turned their backs on centuries ago.

Hecate pushed back her emerald velvet cloak and revealed the most beautiful set of eyes he'd ever seen. They were a peculiar shade of lavender, and the ocean air seemed to electrify them. A huge snake coiled itself around her shoulders and rested on a bed of Hecate's thick black curls. Although the snake seemed at ease, he suspected it would strike with blinding speed should it think its mistress was in danger. Hecate opened her pink cupid's bow mouth and smiled at him. His hair stood on end as her two spirit forms appeared behind her.

He narrowed his eyes. "Why are you here?"

She smiled coyly and said in a drawling, melodic voice, "What? No, 'How nice to see you, Hecate?' or 'It's been so long Hecate. You look amazing!'"

He folded his arms across his chest. He was feeling rather violent, and his hands itched for a weapon. "It's never a simple matter with you, and I lack patience today. Get to the point."

"I heard the plant god's call through the earth. You need help. Someone with magic, perhaps," she continued on as she stated facts. "There are none who can help you with magic as well as I. I removed the local authorities, but I can always bring them back. I suggest you treat me more respectfully."

Here we go again. Hecate and her praise-me-and-worship-me requirements. It was just a matter of time, and she would have him washing her feet.

"Fine then. I'll take you to my leader, and you can talk to him." He expertly passed the buck. Lir could wash her feet all day for all Alex cared. A low, tinkling laugh interrupted his portal chant.

"Silly child," she teased. "You do not need portals when I am here."

She waved a hand, and he was promptly dropped on his ass in the middle of the safe house back in America. He stood up, cracked his neck, and looked across the living room floor to where Finn and Jari were laid out. They groaned loudly, having been dropped just as kindly. He smiled at their pain. Misery loved company.

Mya ran to them, her lips pinched together. As she checked the Guardians for injuries, Alex's mouth cracked into a smile. Her face was beet-red, but he suspected it wasn't from exertion. It was adorable.

"Why's your face so red?" He cocked an eyebrow at her as she refused to meet his gaze.

She fidgeted, twisting her fingers together, and her cheeks turned a deeper shade of crimson. "My face isn't red!"

"Uh-huh, and pigs fly." He climbed to his feet.

She sputtered and was about to respond when Hecate entered her vision. Mya's mouth dropped open in awe.

Gods, he thought, *Hecate's probably eating up the attention like the greedy little witch she is.*

"She's so beautiful." Mya said this *about* Hecate more than *to* her.

"Yep. She's a needy bitch, though," Alex said.

In response, Hecate arched a single brow at him before drawing the breath from his body with her magic juice. She watched demurely as he choked and sputtered, clawing at his throat. Her point made, she released her hold. He gasped for air as he coughed and tried to catch his breath.

"Do we understand each other now, War?" she asked, that same brow arched, this time in question instead of annoyance.

He coughed again and thrust a thumb into the air. "Yep, we're good."

"Excellent. Now fetch me Lir," she ordered, waving him away.

Still a bitch, he thought. "Yes, ma'am." His reply was snide, knowing most women—especially goddesses of a certain age—hated being called ma'am. He exited the room before she took offense.

He found Lir standing outside, waving goodbye to his girlfriend. Kathy, or some shit like that. Whoever she was, she wouldn't last long. Lir never let them linger.

"You haven't broken up with her yet?" Alex asked,

hanging his head and lowering his voice as he came up beside Lir.

Lir grimaced. "I was about to, but she was in my bed. Naked."

That was something Alex could understand. He'd seen many wars fought over beautiful women. Wicked creatures, all of them. He fondly remembered those wars that men had started for women, especially Helen of Troy, the beautiful demigod who made even Aphrodite jealous.

Why would any man deny a naked and willing woman? He clapped Lir on the shoulder and let out a dry laugh. "Totally understand, bro."

They stared up at the night sky in companionable silence. Lir was the reason he'd joined the Guardians. Lir was his brother in every way but blood. He would die for him, and he couldn't leave him alone. Especially now, when Lir would need him most. Zeus was losing patience and becoming reckless. An epic battle lay ahead of them.

This thought brought him back to the reason he sought Lir in the first place. He broke the silence by clearing his throat. "Hecate is here. She's offering aid and wants to speak with you."

Lir glanced at him in surprise.

Alex weighed the options. "Do we take her offer? You know she comes with a hefty price tag."

Lir sighed and closed his eyes with his face tipped toward the heavens. "Yes, she does, but we need her. Let's see what she has to say and what the cost will be this time."

They found her in the living room, perched delicately on an armchair, making herself comfortable. The goddess looked fragile and almost mortal sitting there like that. The visage, however, was ruined by her spooky spirit forms roaming about.

"Hello, Hecate." Lir greeted her with a forced smile.

She smiled in response. "My favorite god of the oceans and what lies beneath, I told you we would meet again." She held out a hand that Alex knew was softer than silk.

For a moment, he wondered what those hands would feel like across his skin, along his chest, grabbing his dick—

Lir's voice snapped him back to reality. He cleared his throat and adjusted his trousers, ashamed to even think of Hecate that way.

"We need an experienced witch, that is correct. She's a goddess"—he gestured over to Mya—"but doesn't know how to access her powers. We don't even know what type of goddess she is."

Hecate smiled at Mya, and as she did, her spirits started circling the girl, assessing her. Mya turned pale—a far departure from her red, flustered face from earlier. She remained still as they swirled around her, leaving small wisps of smoke wherever they grazed her body.

Hecate's eyes narrowed as she spoke, the same way a scholar might squint at an ancient tome. "She is a goddess, indeed. She has been reborn." With unwavering confidence, she added, "I can help you."

"At what cost?" Lir asked. "Whatever it is, *I'll* pay for it and not Mya. Is that clear?"

"Oh, yes. Crystal clear." A spirit form's hand slithered down Lir's cheek.

Scary ass bitch. Can't she just move her own body? Alex thought.

"Zeus is concocting a war against the mortals who forsook him," Hecate said. "We will not allow that to happen. If he wins, all will perish. Gods, humans, and everything in between." She spoke prophetically and brought her eyes to meet Lir's. "I want to live. Don't you?"

Alex wondered what game she was playing today.

"Yes," Lir said, "but you still haven't explained what your price is."

Hecate spread her enticing lips into a playful smile. Her spirit forms floated back toward her, and in unison, they said, "When you have saved humanity from Zeus, I simply want acknowledgement." She raised her brow again as her smile faltered. "I want them to believe again. In me and in magic."

Alex knew it wasn't that simple, but what choice did they have?

"Okay, I agree to your terms," Lir said.

She offered a genuine smile this time, and quicker than a flash of light, she sliced an opalescent blade through both their palms and smeared them together. She stared into his turquoise eyes. "A divine agreement bound by divine blood." After a moment, she clapped her hands together and barked some orders to no one in particular. "Now, I will need sage, chalk, a chalice, and candles."

☉☾☉

MYA

MYA FELT ON edge as she watched the goddess work. Magic seemed unpredictable, and until a few days ago, it didn't even exist to her. If someone had told her she was a goddess then, she would've laughed in their face.

Hecate's spirits ripped the rug from the floor and tossed it to the side while Hecate crouched down and drew a large circle with the chalk. The goddess looked up at Mya. "Now, Mya, I will need you to sit inside the circle, please."

Mya did as instructed.

"Jari, will you be a dear and light the candles now?" Hecate directed more than asked.

Jari carried the burning incense to each candle and lit them with a covered hand.

Hecate turned her lavender eyes to Finn. "Did you collect the sage?" she asked.

He handed her a dried and bundled sage stick, and she replied with a grin.

"Most excellent. This is of premium quality, Finn."

He hit her with his mesmerizing smile and a little bow. "Had you expected any less, my lady?"

Mya groaned. He was an epic flirt. Hecate simply patted his cheek, unaffected by his boyish charm. Lir handed a chalice to Hecate, and she accepted absently.

"Ow!" Mya shrieked. Hecate had drawn a blade across her palm when she wasn't looking.

"Oh, do not be such a pansy, dear," Hecate continued. "I just needed a bit of blood."

"A warning would have been nice," Mya muttered.

Hecate walked away with the chalice of blood.

Mya pressed a hand to her wound, staunching the blood flow. "Just a little bit of blood, my ass."

Hecate began chanting. The lights burned out and shrouded the room in darkness. Air turned still and stagnant, each breath feeling thicker than the one before it. Mya's heart pounded in her ears. She watched as her blood rose from the chalice and circled around her, turning a shimmery black. She collapsed onto the floor, her eyes rolling back in her head as she lost consciousness.

SHE WOKE to the sound of running water. *Did someone leave a faucet on?* She gathered her bearings and looked around. She was in a cave, the rough walls around her holding tightly to moisture from the air. She stood and found herself walking toward the sounds of the stream.

Somehow unaffected by the darkness, she found the moving water with ease. Upon arriving, she felt compelled to drink. She scooped the liquid in her hands and gulped it down. It cooled her stomach as it enveloped her within a vision.

It was her, but not her.

Dark hair, large brown eyes, and a petite frame. The other her wore a dark, flowing dress and was veiled in shadows, as if they were her friends.

This must be the past life Hecate mentioned.

Her doppelgänger smiled at her and spoke. "You are me, and I am you. Reborn. Reincarnated, if you will. I am your eternal spirit, and this is your spirit realm." The other her sounded different . . . wiser, perhaps?

"Who are we?" Mya asked.

"We are Nyx, the goddess of the night."

"I thought gods were immortal. Some said they've been alive for centuries. How did we die? Why were we reincarnated again?" She needed answers.

"I don't know why we were reincarnated." Her ancient voice felt small for a moment, as if not knowing something scared her. "However, I can tell you how we died." The spirit paused and sighed. "To put it simply, Zeus is afraid of us. He justly fears we are more powerful than him." She paused briefly before continuing with a thick sadness to her voice. "When he decided on his war, he convinced one of my own children to kill me."

Mya gasped and covered her mouth with both hands. "I'm so sorry. That's horrible."

Nyx looked at her with sorrowful eyes, but Mya realized she didn't feel the same sadness. She was Nyx, but not quite Nyx? Yes, she was still Mya, and now she would be Mya, goddess of the night.

"Zeus killed you because you're stronger than him?"

Nyx nodded at her.

"Why is he at war with the gods?"

Nyx stood up, black shadows trailing her. "That is a complicated answer, and one we do not have time for. I will tell you this . . . Zeus wants all humans killed. He wants to create a new batch of humans that will worship him properly. Correctly." She enunciated. "Not all the gods agree with his madness, and I was one of the dissenters."

A war among the gods sounded terrifying and dangerous. What might happen to the humans in the middle of this war? Despair washed over her. There was no way they could all survive this. She was certain some of them would die, if not all of them.

When had she started referring to the humans as "them" and not "us"? She pushed that thought aside. She now understood why the gods wanted to stop Zeus, but how could they? He was the King of the gods for a reason, right? The Greek King, from what she understood, but still a king—a leader. He had to be incredibly powerful and calculating to some extent.

"How do I defeat him?" Mya asked with a newfound reason.

Nyx thought for a moment. "I cannot tell you, for I do not know." A look of puzzlement clouded her features. "I knew the answer once. I was always watching Zeus and his little soldiers, hiding in my shadows and lurking at the edge of light. I was biding my time, but for some reason, those memories will not come back to me." She balled her fists.

Ok, great, Mya thought. She had one more question for this Nyx.

"What about my powers? How do I access them?" She glanced down at her hands and flexed her fingers in hopes something would happen. Nothing did.

Her spirit form reached a hand toward her head, and she winced as the ethereal fingers dug into her mind. They groped gently, but it was still uncomfortable.

Nyx frowned and looked into Mya's eyes. "It seems your powers have been bound. A spell placed at birth." The spirit of Nyx seemed angry as she started pacing, and her shadows followed in restless agitation.

Mya furrowed her brow. "How do I unbind my powers? Can I?"

Nyx looked at her with stars shining in her eyes. It was pretty, but also unsettling. Her voice was almost inhuman as she spoke again. "You will need an extremely powerful witch to reverse it."

With that, Mya was yanked from her spirit realm. She woke on the floor of the safe house living room. Lir's face hung over hers, his thick black brows pinched together, and his normal scowl firmly in place.

"Dude, personal space," she said, pushing her hand against rock hard muscle as she shoved him away.

He still hovered, so she waved her hand. After a moment, he flashed a heartfelt smile, and the effect caused her to blush. She could blame the red tinge to her cheeks on a side effect of the spirit world.

He stood and offered her a hand. "I was worried. I'm glad you're ok."

As she took his hand and stood up, her head began to

swim. She stumbled into him. He scooped her up, sat on the couch, and settled her into his lap, cradling her like a small child. And—though she hated to admit it—she loved it. Yes, she would blame her flushed face on the whole ordeal.

"I told the brute you were just fine," Hecate said, exasperated.

"You'll have to forgive me for not trusting you, Hecate," Lir said. "It isn't in your nature to be forthcoming."

She shrugged, unbothered by his insult. "Tell me, child, what did you see?" the witch inquired as she stood in front of Mya.

"I was in some kind of spirit realm, but inside my head, I think. Nyx was there. She's my spirit. The goddess of the night. I'm her, but not quite."

Hecate smiled at her, and the effect made the goddess even more beautiful. "You are a goddess of the night? That is good. Excellent, actually." She said this to herself more than to the room. With a chuckle, she said, "You will be strong. With your divine powers unlocked, we might have a chance at defeating Zeus."

"That's the thing," Mya interrupted with a squinted grimace. "Nyx can't release my powers. She told me a spell was placed on me at birth, binding them." She paused, but Hecate continued staring at her, prompting her for more information. "She said I need an exceptionally powerful witch to break the spell. That's you, right? You can help me?"

Hecate stepped back and took a moment to respond. "I could, yes. But I won't."

CHAPTER ELEVEN

MYA

Mya was confused. Wasn't that what this whole damn thing was about?

"Why?" Lir demanded. He stroked Mya's dark hair as he spoke. The act was so soothing, she considered falling asleep in his arms. Let the real gods handle this mess.

"The kind of magic it would take to unbind her powers would weaken me considerably, and frankly, I do not trust any of you to protect me while I am weak." She held up her hands. "No offense."

"What do you suggest we do, then? We need her," Finn said.

Mya glanced over to see him seated on the couch with his boots crossed over each other.

Hecate pursed her lips. "We will need a full coven. Together, they can help her."

The Summer Solstice! Mya turned her head to look at Lir. "Remember when you had us doing research on witches?"

"Yes," he answered with slightly narrowed eyes.

"The Summer Solstice is in two months. A local coven, the Anderson family, typically visits Alki Beach every year to celebrate. They invite other covens and burn things, eat food, and perform rituals to celebrate the sun on the longest day of the year."

Lir stared at her. "You found all that out?"

She smirked back. "Yes, I did. Just call me the genius goddess."

He offered her a small smile. "Did you find any info on the prophecy?"

Hecate cocked her hip. "Prophecy, you say? Care to explain that to the only one here who understands magic?"

Lir detailed the events with the deceased witch and the prophecy she spoke out of her dead, floating head.

Hecate chewed over that bit and spoke up. "The first part of the prophecy already came true. The one who is night will be found." She turned those peculiar, electrified, lavender eyes on Mya.

Mya nodded. The magical witch was right.

"Nyx is known for having abilities with prophetic powers. Perhaps that was Mya? Could she have accessed her powers somehow?" Hecate was once again speaking mainly to herself. "Especially, if she felt scared or pressured, some spells will allow the person to access their powers in dire situations. I wonder if whoever blocked Mya thought they were protecting her somehow." The goddess directed her attention back to Mya. "Do you know your parents?"

"No, I grew up in foster homes. I never knew my parents. I've always assumed I was an orphan."

"Well, that complicates things. I suppose we will need the coven, after all. I will stay here until then." She paused for a moment. "Yes, that is best." She looked up at Lir. "I will need a comfortable room to sleep in. I expect you can provide me with one?"

He gave a sheepish look and deferred. "Um, we only have one guest room, and it's currently occupied by Mya."

Hecate waved her arms dramatically. "Well, it is ridiculous that you only have one guest room in a safe house protected by Guardians!"

She did have a point there.

"I can give up my room. It's fine," Mya conceded. "I'm used to sleeping on couches anyway."

Lir frowned at her. "I don't want you to be uncomfortable. You need more rest than any of us do." Lir looked toward the rest of the room. "Finn prefers to sleep outside most nights. He can give up his room."

Finn's face turned red, and he balled his fists. "Bollocks! I am not giving up my room for Hecate! Besides, Queen Witch wouldn't like my room anyway!" His Irish accent was more obvious when angry. "Make Jari or Alex give up their rooms."

Lir looked at them, a question in his eyes. They shook their heads no.

Lir scrubbed a hand down his face. "You're all a bunch of children!" he yelled. "Mya can have my room, then. I'll take the damn couch." He stood abruptly, dropping her on the floor.

Ow, she thought.

"I need a cigarette!" he said in a gruff voice and stormed away. Like a hurricane, water swirled around him, drenching the floor.

He's letting me sleep in his room! She could snoop through all his stuff, and he wouldn't be the wiser. This was perfect. He did seem upset, though, and she wondered if she should follow him. Maybe he could use a friend? *No,* she mused, *he would likely bite my head off. Best to let sleeping dogs lie.*

Hecate stretched and, on a half-yawn, said, "Mya, I had best retire now. Care to show me to my quarters?"

"Sure." She stood up from the puddle Lir had summoned and led Hecate up the stairs to her room. "Here we are. This is your room." She directed Hecate in with a wave of her arm. The goddess looked around in disgust.

"This is . . . cozy," she said with a sneer.

Mya rolled her eyes. She loved this room and thought it was great. It was the best room she'd been able to call her own in a long time. Granted, she'd only slept in it for a few nights. Still, she felt a little offended, having given up her room for Hecate and the witch didn't even like it. Her ire only lasted a moment once she remembered she'd be sleeping in Lir's room.

She collected her things and headed back downstairs, ready to be away from the goddess of magic. She had a way of making a person feel a little off.

Jari stood at the foot of the stairs, her dark hair loose around her shoulders and a Cheshire grin painted on her face. She gave Mya a wink. "Let's go out."

Mya considered it for a moment. "Where?"

"I know of a club. A hot, dirty one." She wiggled her hips at the word "dirty."

Mya gave a girlish laugh. She could use a nice distraction, and a club sounded perfect. When was the last time she'd gone out? When was the last time she'd even been *invited* out?

"Okay," she said. "But I have nothing to wear."

Jari shot her a wicked smile. "I can help with that."

Oh no. Who knew what the serpentine goddess would dress her in. Based on the wardrobe she'd seen so far, she was more than a little concerned. Before she could respond, Jari dragged her upstairs to her tidy little room.

She dove into her closet and came out holding what seemed to be strips of fabric. She thrust them at Mya. "Here, try these on."

Yikes.

She pulled on the first dress and had to admit . . . she looked good in it. The midnight-blue satin felt as smooth as a second skin. It was barely long enough to conceal her ample ass, and she had a feeling this was a no-underwear dress. No bra, either, considering the way it clung to her curves. She turned around again to check out her butt. She could see her panty lines. With reluctance, she shimmied her bikini cut underwear down her legs, grateful she had shaved.

She pulled on a pair of Jari's strappy black stilettos. This was dangerous. Mya was accident-prone, and she could just imagine how sexy she would look when walking around in these things while teetering like a toddler and falling down every two seconds.

Jari emerged from the bathroom and surveyed her. She let out a little whistle. "Dang, girl! Looking good, sexy mama." She was being catcalled! "I knew this dress was perfect for you."

She smiled at Jari. "Thanks for the dress and for taking me out. This is really nice."

Jari shrugged. "Get used to it, sister! It's me and you against the boys."

"Damn right, bitch!"

She took a moment to check out Jari. Black liner rimmed her eerie hazel eyes. She wore a mini dress, too, but hers was black, spandex, and strapped around her body like something out of a bondage getup. Mya was curious how she got into it and how she planned to get out of it. Jari's large breasts threatened to spill over the top.

Meanwhile, Mya's small breasts sat in place, perfectly covered.

Jari was beautiful and if she hadn't liked her so much, she would have been a little jealous.

"You look great, too," Mya said. "Men are gonna eat out of the palm of your hand." She finished with a wink.

"I hope not. I'd much prefer for them to eat my pussy."

"Oh my god!" Mya sputtered.

Jari smacked her arm playfully. "Don't be such a Virgin Mary, Mya." Jari stopped and slid her gaze over Mya's body. "Wait, you aren't a virgin, are you?"

"What? No!" Mya cried and gave Jari an indignant look. "I just don't go willy-nilly, talking about men . . . you know."

Jari paused for a second, considering Mya with scrutiny. "But they have, right?"

"Yes," Mya said reluctantly. She didn't want to talk about her sex life anymore. That would lead to another blushing fit as she thought about a certain sexy god. *Does Lir go down on women? Oh god, shut it, you dirty slut,* she internally yelled at herself.

"Oh, good. We can still be friends then," Jari said with relief.

"You're so bad, Jari."

"You'll be more sexually open when you get to my age, too."

"Just how old are you?" Mya asked with an evil grin.

"I was there when Pompeii was destroyed, when the Romans conquered Greece, and when Persia became a new dynasty."

"What?" Mya shrieked with wide eyes.

Jari waved away her shock. "I lose track of time all too

easily these days. I can't even remember history all that well." Jari sighed and looked up at Mya with a sparkle in her eye. "Now sit. We need to do your hair and makeup." Jari shoved her into a chair.

AN HOUR and a full pound of make-up later, she and Jari headed downstairs. They passed Finn and Alex on the way out, who both whistled at them.

Finn gave the goddesses an appreciative look and asked, "Where are you fine little ladies headed?"

"Avalon," Jari said.

Finn showed a wide, irresistible smile. "Aurora's club? Let me and Alex go? Please?" He placed his hands together in a prayer pose and gazed at Jari with puppy dog eyes.

Jari chuckled. "You can come, but do *not* be a cock blocker, got it?"

"No problem. I'll leave you alone the whole time. Promise." Finn jumped up from the couch.

Mya noticed Alex staring at her legs. At least she hoped it was her legs.

His voice was deep and husky. "I can't make the same promises." His eyes trailed up Mya's body, ending at her eyes. He licked his lips.

Jari threw a protective arm around Mya. "In your dreams, Alex. Mya has a hard-on for Lir."

Finn chuckled.

"Your face is turning red," Jari pointed out. "Is it because you're thinking of Lir right now?"

"No," Mya lied as she felt the heat on her cheeks.

Alex's leer turned predatory. "The best way to get over a crush is to find another. Just saying."

"I'm so done with this conversation." Mya headed outside, needing some fresh air.

Of course, Lir was there.

He strode up to the door, soaked to the bone with the sea. Droplets sparkled in his raven hair, and water glistened off his perfectly sculpted abs. Her vagina tightened in response to the near-voyeuristic scene in front of her.

Traitorous bitch. she mentally scolded her body. *Fine, I have a "hard-on" for Lir.* She could admit that to herself, but she had decided she wouldn't sleep with him. The man was a total jackass.

He stopped and studied her carefully. He was checking her out! His gaze roved over her body, lingering in certain places.

His hazy look cleared, as if he had just become aware of how long they'd been silently appraising each other. He cleared his throat. "You look beautiful. Where are you headed?"

Mya squeaked out a response. "A club with Jari, Finn, and Alex." She tried to make her tone sound cool and aloof, but she was ninety percent sure she'd failed.

He shook his head and sighed. "Be careful. I'll set my room up for you, and you can just head there when you get back." He gave her a cocky grin. "You know where it is."

She felt her cheeks flame again.

"Thank you," she said.

He nodded and headed inside, that stupid grin still on his face.

CHAPTER TWELVE

JARI

J ari inhaled the thick scent of sweat, sex, and alcohol. It intoxicated her. Her libido swelled into a rhythmic tempo to dance in time with the music blaring out of the speakers. It was a pulsing, thumping beat that reached her to her core. She gazed around the room, lingering here and there as she spotted writhing bodies on the dance floor. There were even couples sprinkled around the various corners having sex.

Avalon was a free-for-all place for supernatural beings—a club where they could be their truest selves and have a good time. The club's owner didn't frown on public sex. Or anything sexual, really. Aurora was a sex goddess, after all.

Jari eyed Mya standing next to her. She kept pulling her dress down to cover her assets. Jari couldn't understand why. She looked great. Mya stopped tugging down her dress and crossed her arms instead. No one was going to approach her with such don't-fucking-talk-to-me body language. She needed to loosen up.

"Relax, Mya. This is a safe place. Just let loose and have fun," Jari said as she leaned closer to speak into Mya's ear.

The new goddess dropped her arms, feigning relaxation. She was going to have to work on her a bit more.

On Jari's other side, Alex rubbed his hands together in anticipation. He offered a feral-looking grin and cocked a brow. "See ya, losers. I'm going hunting."

He headed straight for a group of girls in the middle of the dance floor and dived in. They giggled, rubbing his arms and ogling him. One of the bolder girls grabbed his ass, giving it a hard squeeze. Alex didn't care. He probably already had his hand halfway into one of their pants.

Finn was asking around, likely looking for Aurora. Smart guy.

Jari looked back at Mya and beckoned with her finger. "Come on. Let's hit the bar and grab some drinks."

Mya looked relieved to have something to do other than stand there. "Ok," she agreed.

They walked past the black high-top tables and the red leather-backed booths lining the edges of the club. Jari spotted Aurora near the bar. Her auburn curls were styled to perfection.

Jari shoved her way through the throng of drunken idiots, their sweat-soaked bodies colliding with her at every turn. Aurora spotted her and launched herself into Jari's arms. Finn walked up behind the sex goddess, his mouth pinched in frustration at Jari having found Aurora first. She stuck out her tongue, teasing him.

"Jari, I've missed you! Where have you been? What have you been up to? We must catch up at once," Aurora said in one breath, then ushered her to the bar with a gentle push. The goddess was so excited, she didn't even notice Finn until they got to the counter. She snatched him into a big hug, squeezing tightly. He stuck out his tongue at Jari that time, returning the favor.

"Finn," she said, "I missed you too." Aurora stroked his chest in an intimate gesture.

He was wearing what he called his get-the-ladies t-shirt. He called it this because it was a size you could only find at Baby Gap and showed off his rippling muscles.

Finn smiled down at Aurora, placed both hands in a caress on either side of her face, and kissed her. Thoroughly. He gently nipped her lips before sliding his tongue into her mouth. He slipped one hand to the back of her head and deepened the kiss.

I should probably look away, Jari thought. It was an intimate exchange that reminded her of the times Finn had kissed her like that.

Aurora let out a deep, sexy moan and broke off the kiss. She looked up at Finn and tucked a blond lock behind his ear. "Later, cowboy," she crooned in a seductive voice before turning her attention to Mya. "And who is this?" Her tone brightened, as if she wasn't just locked in a heated smooch. Aurora was unique that way.

"This is Mya. She's a goddess of the night." Jari responded for Mya, who looked a little flushed by the rather sexual escapade she'd just witnessed. "Under the protection of the Guardians, of course."

Aurora addressed Mya directly, looking her over. "Oh, I had a feeling you were something like that. I never met Nyx personally, but you do look very much like the drawings I've seen."

Jari assessed Aurora's reaction as the sex goddess continued speaking to Mya.

"Did you change your identity?"

The gods were known to do that. You didn't remain the same person when you've lived for centuries upon centuries.

"No, I was reincarnated," Mya said.

Aurora reared her head back like someone had slapped her. "I've never encountered a reincarnated goddess before. That is . . . interesting."

"I suppose you could say that," Mya said with a grimace.

Aurora clapped her hands together, her many bracelets jingling. "Well, that's enough melancholy. You stop that right now. Aurora is going to fix you right up with a nice drink." She leaned in closer and said, "On the house, of course." She ushered the bartender toward them with a crook of her finger.

He sauntered over, his walk reminding Jari of a big cat prowling for a meal. He was tall. Judging by the way his head danced with the hanging lights, she guessed he was well over six feet. His shoulders were strong and broad, and his chest was impeccably toned. He had long, straight, jet-black hair, and his wicked green eyes held a hint of what he might do to a woman, given the chance.

Jari naturally wondered what he might be like in the sack. She'd put her godly status on the line to bet he was a treat to behold. He looked like he knew how to pound into a girl for longer than two minutes.

She gave him her full stare and arched her back to put her ample breasts on full display. "Well, hello there, sexy," she purred.

The bartender barely glanced at her before turning to Aurora. "Friend of yours?" he asked dryly.

Fine, she thought. *I'll find someone else, then. He doesn't know what he's missing.* She was gorgeous, and she knew it.

Aurora glared at him and dropped her tone to something more authoritative. "Yes, she is my friend and my guest, Gabriel." She motioned over to Alex, still enmeshed with the women on the dance floor. "Be polite. Especially if you see Alex. I would much prefer it if he didn't take offense and rip up my club as he tossed around your bloody carcass."

Gabriel cocked his head and laughed. "And why should I be afraid of this Alex?"

"He's one of the Guardians of Terra. They all are, in fact." Aurora gestured to us. "Alex is the god of war, in the flesh."

The bartender paled and looked back at Jari with renewed interest. *Bastard.* She'd make him want her and would make sure to parade around the bar with her newest boy toy. She'd have to find another scary looking dude. That would be a challenge, but she hated weak men, and they hated her, too.

Aurora placed a petite hand on Jari's shoulder. "I apologize on Gabe's behalf. He's an incubus demon, and he gets a lot of attention." She gestured to the atmosphere of the club to emphasize her point. "He grows tired of it. I suppose I can level with him on that." Aurora finished with a sigh.

Fuck, an incubus? She'd been waiting years to find one, and now he was standing right there! *What would sex be like with an incubus?*

No, she would stick to her plan and make him beg for her. He'd offended her, and she wasn't one to let it go. Plus, to make an incubus beg . . . well, that would be delightful to watch.

She glanced up to meet his gaze, staring into his green, swirling irises that seemed to suck her right in. Those eyes said, come to me, and damn, she wanted to. He slid a drink to her and winked.

"Mmm, sexy bastard," she muttered.

He smirked and gave her his back, which infuriated and intrigued her more. She felt a hand on her arm and regretfully turned her gaze from Gabe's immaculate ass. It was Mya, pulling her away.

86

"Come on, leave the sexy incubus demon alone. Plenty of incubus demons in the sea." She paused. "I think?"

Jari had to laugh at her newfound friend's attempt to cheer her up. It was a good one, although incubi *were* pretty hard to come by. They ditched Finn and headed to the dance floor for some real fun.

৩ষ্ঠ

MYA

Exhausted, Mya pushed her way through the dancing, writhing bodies and searched for an empty table—which wasn't easy. She passed a door that she suspected was a room. Curious to see if she might find peace and quiet there, she opened the door. She couldn't have been more wrong.

Mya stared for a full minute with her mouth gaping open.
What the hell?

She saw creatures of all kinds—things she didn't know existed and couldn't identify. There were plenty of weird, animal-like limbs and oddly shaped heads with inhuman features, but the really disturbing part was the sexual display. Feet! She gagged a little as one creature raked his long tongue across another creature's human looking foot. Disgusted and feeling a little nauseated, she turned and jumped ship.

Slamming the door firmly behind her, she shuffled away until she found an empty booth to sink into. She peeled off her heels and sighed with relief. Jari could exhaust a girl with her insane endurance and insatiable appetite for dancing. Mya was tired. She wanted to go home, climb in bed, and relax. She thought back to when Lir held her on the couch, and she sighed. She missed him.

Why, why, why? She didn't want to feel lust for him, but she did.

She couldn't remember the last time she had wanted a man so badly. Though . . . he wasn't really a man.

She'd had a continuous string of bad luck when it came to men. Her first real crush in high school realized he was gay after they kissed. She moved on after that and made friends in her new foster home. It was a decent one . . . before the couple split up and decided it was best not to foster kids anymore. With her first broken heart, she was forced to move again.

She met a nice guy during that period and even gained her first real best friend. She lived there for two years, which was the longest she'd been in any home. She was at the highest peak of her new life when everything fell apart. Her boyfriend cheated on her with her best friend and they, of course, broke up. That hurt more than anything she'd felt before. She lost her first best friend and her first boyfriend at the same time. By the time she was sixteen, she was living on her own and found herself in the clutches of an abusive asshole.

He cheated on her, coming home smelling like other women and pretending nothing happened. She didn't dare confront him, either. That would've led to him beating on her. She shuddered as she fought against her roiling emotions.

"Hello?"

She opened her eyes and found a man sitting across from her. She squinted, surveying him briefly. *Is there a light around his head?* she wondered.

He was cute, with messy blond hair and large brown eyes. His kind gaze made her want to feel safe with him, though she wasn't sure if she should. His charming smile disarmed her, but could she trust it? It was nothing like Lir's grin—

dangerous to her libido, but still filled with safety and sincerity.

"Are you ok?" he asked, his voice deep. "You seem a little upset."

"Yes, I'm fine."

He continued to run his gaze over her body, and she determined he didn't plan to leave anytime soon.

"Just trying to relax for a minute. Dancing got me a little tired, that's all." She forced a smile. She was still a bit rattled from her little trip down memory lane.

His smile brightened. "Oh, yeah. I get that. I'm not a dancing man, myself." He was beginning his little game of flirtation. "What's your name?"

She gave him a once over, decided he was harmless enough, and held out her hand. "Mya. And you are?"

He took her hand in his and kissed her knuckles. She felt her mood lighten, and she giggled like a schoolgirl.

He almost purred his response. "It's a pleasure to meet you, Mya. You may call me Mikail." He raised his big brown eyes to hers. "May I ask what a nice girl like you is doing in an infamous sex club?"

Sex club? She thought this was just a club for the supernatural. Maybe he said that because of Aurora.

She squeaked out a reply. "My friends brought me here."

He quirked his brow. "The Guardians?" When she looked up with surprise, he added, "I saw you with them earlier."

Ah, so he was familiar with them. Maybe he knew Aurora personally. "Yes. I'm with them."

His eyes widened. She couldn't tell if it was desire or shock. "Are you a goddess?"

She didn't know the protocol here, but they seemed to be in a pretty open environment, so she felt comfortable responding. "Yes. I am." She said it simply, though the words felt odd coming out of her mouth. She wasn't about to spill all her goddess secrets—assuming she had them—and how little she knew to this stranger.

He caught the hint and splayed his hands in the air, as if in surrender. "You're quite safe with me. I'm a Seraphim." When she didn't respond, he explained. "An angel, and I swear on my wings, I won't harm you."

That's nice, she thought, but she didn't believe it wholly. On the surface, he appeared nice, but like his disarming smile, a little *too* nice. She was curious, though. A real-life angel sat in front of her.

"Tell me more about . . . being an angel. I've never met one before."

"There are multiple levels of angels. I'm an angel of the highest order. One of the seraphim. I work directly with the One True God."

Mya opened her mouth to ask more questions just as Jari appeared with a tray of shots in her hand. She sank down in the booth next to Mya and handed her a glass.

"Drink up!"

Mya complied and drank the glass in one gulp, her head spinning as she did.

Man, these gods like to drink!

Jari looked at Mikail and handed him a glass. "You too, angel boy. It's time to par-tay!"

Mikail chuckled. "I don't drink, but thanks."

"That's cool, you don't have to drink." Jari drained the glass she'd offered to Mikail.

"Mikail was telling me all about the angels, and I'm interested, so shhh." Mya placed a wobbly finger over Jari's lips and released a bubble of laughter.

Jari swatted her finger away. "Go ahead. I won't interrupt. Promise."

Mya looked back at Mikail and shuffled through her memories. What had she wanted to ask? "What are the other types of angels? You said there are others, right?"

Mikail lifted his brow in amusement. "Yes, there are many levels. Cherubim, for example, they sort of"—he waved his hand—"serve God directly."

"Like his maid or something?"

"Yes, exactly. Then there's the lowest tier of angels. They watch over humans and protect them from death when it's not their time. They also watch over people who are grieving or need help."

Mya leaned closer to him, intrigued. "What about the archangels? I mean, everyone's heard of them, right? What do they do?"

"They're the most popular because one of the bibles wrote them as powerful beings. They're also the only types of angels who allow humans to know they exist. I suspect they've gained feelings for the humans, and that's why they allowed them such knowledge."

"Why do you think they gained feelings for the humans?"

Mikail pursed his lips. "Because they're in charge of the guardian angels and spend all their time on Earth, watching and interacting with the humans."

Finn stalked through the crowd and joined them at the booth. Mikail slid over in the seat and ended up next to Mya as Finn sank into his old seat across the table.

He looked over at them with a huge smile. "What's up? You guys having fun?"

Mya laughed. She loved that Finn always made her smile. "Not as much fun as you seem to be having. What happened to Aurora?"

He shrugged. "She had stuff to do. Running a club is hard work, apparently. Who knew?"

"What's up, Cass?"

"My name is Mikai—"

"Who's Cass?" Jari asked.

Finn smirked. "Cass is the angel on Supernatural. It's only the best TV show ever. If you haven't watched it, you need to."

Jari shrugged at him, and they all started talking and chatting amicably. Mya sat back and watched the whole thing. She was really starting to like the Guardians. They were fun to be around, always interesting, and they didn't make her feel like an outsider.

She started thinking through everything Mikail said about the angels—that the angels watch out for the humans. She always figured that was untrue, considering how difficult her life and the lives of others had been. She figured if God was real, he didn't really care what happened to the humans. But maybe he did care, and if so, did that mean he would help them defeat Zeus?

"Mikail?"

"Yes?" he asked, whipping his sandy blond head back toward her.

"You said you work directly with God. Does that mean you actually talk to him?"

"Well, no not really . . ."

"That's 'cause he's a faker." Finn leaned back against the booth with a smirk.

"What do you mean?" Mikail spoke in a calm voice, but his still body said his actions hinged on what Finn said next.

"I mean, he pretends that he's the only god and that he gave humans life. Both statements are untrue, making him a faker." Finn belched.

Mikail blinked in disbelief. "The One True God calls

himself so because he's the strongest of the gods. He's the reason everything exists."

Finn pointed in Mikail's face. "Nope. Zeus created everything except your breed and the demon creatures."

"Zeus did not create humans. *He* is the faker." Mikail growled. Embers burned through his eyes as not one, but three pairs of snow-white wings exploded from his back. They pinned Mya against the booth with the force of their expanse.

Mya stared at them reverently.

Alex appeared in front of them, amber eyes blazing as smoke billowed from his nostrils. His chest puffed out, and his fists clenched in anger. The dragon tattoo on his shoulder swirled and moved around on his skin. *"You hurt Mya!"*

CHAPTER THIRTEEN

MYA

Bemused, Mya inspected her body and wondered what he was talking about. Blood trickled from a small cut on her shoulder. Alex had been right, but she felt fine. He didn't need to overreact. She was about to say as much when Alex lifted the table with one hand and threw it against the wall. Some of the club patrons screamed and ran away. Mya understood their fear.

Finn rose from his seat. "What the hell did you do that for?"

Alex ignored him and continued to stare at Mikail with venom in his eyes. Mikail unfurled his wings and flew out of the booth. He landed behind Alex and kicked him in the back. The god of war spun around and swung a meaty fist into Mikail's jaw. It sounded like a crack of lightning.

Holy shit! Alex is fucking strong.

Mikail reared back from the blow and spat blood in Alex's face. The remaining crowd started backing away. Some ran screaming, and some moved into the corners of the room to watch. A Satyr who was nearby serving drinks—Mya recently learned that's what the half-goat looking creatures were—grumbled something about hotheaded gods and stupid angels.

Mikail's wings propelled him into the air. "This isn't about me hitting Mya. I barely scratched her. What's your real problem?"

Alex leaned back and roared, smoke billowing out of his nostrils and mouth. Mikail dodged the smoke, throwing kicks faster than Alex could catch them.

"Let's be honest. You're not mad at me for hurting her, which was an accident, by the way. You just wanted an excuse to hit me. You've been dreaming of this day since I stole your girl an entire century ago. Get over it."

Mya looked at Jari. "You need to tell me about this girlfriend. Also, why is smoke coming out of his nose?"

Jari threw an arm over her shoulder. "I will definitely tell you about the girlfriend. As for the other thing, the smoke is from his altered god-form. He turns into a dragon if he needs to. He rarely does because dragons are huge, and the transformation will weaken him."

Mya opened her mouth to ask more questions about this god-form thing when she spotted Alex smashing Mikail onto the granite countertops.

Mya jolted in fear. "He's going to kill him!"

"Nah, angels can't die, and he'll heal anyway," Jari said.

She attempted to process this information and piece together what she knew from the old mythology she'd read in high school. Still, she felt a little guilty. Alex was brutal in his onslaught, and she felt for the angel—whether he would die or not.

Alex heaved Mikail's body over his shoulder and swung him toward a wall. Mikail's ruined wings stirred, but they couldn't stop the impending impact. The plaster fell apart from the blow as the lights flickered and the music died out. The club became so still and quiet, you could hear a pin drop.

Mikail pulled himself out of the rubble and stood to face Alex once more. His wings were torn and bloody, his jeans reduced to tatters. Drywall peppered his hair. Alex heaved a breath, faced down the angel, then turned and ripped apart a bar stool.

Jari changed from nonchalant to alarmed within a breath, her face paling.

Mya stood up from the booth. "Alex! Stop it! You're acting crazy!" she shouted while walking toward him.

Finn threw vines from his hands. They flew across the room and twisted themselves around Alex. He struggled for a moment before ripping the plant matter apart with his bare fists. He turned to Mikail with the barstool's central steel rod in hand and lunged. Finn threw himself on Alex and shoved him back. After a bit of a struggle, Finn sat him down on a stool.

"Calm down, you bloody fool!" Finn yelled.

Alex, still high on adrenaline and rage, shrugged him off and started pacing.

Mya felt something enter the room—a calm but exciting change to the air. She turned toward the stairs. Aurora appeared and strolled over to Alex. She oozed sex appeal. Even Mya felt her effects, like tingles spreading down her body and landing between her legs. The tingles turned into a warm caress that made Mya feel a bit uncomfortable.

Aurora must be using her powers, she thought.

Aurora inhaled. The sound of her breath grabbed Alex and turned his attention to her. He met her with two long strides and snatched her by the waist.

"There, there, big guy," she murmured into his hair. "Everything's fine."

To Mya's surprise, he grabbed her by the ass, picked her up, and kissed her. The goddess wrapped her legs around his body and kissed him back.

Oh my god.

Jari laughed. "Dirty slut. She's gonna have the boys fighting when they come home."

"Why?"

"Because Finn is in love with Aurora but . . . she doesn't love him back." Jari frowned. "Not like that, anyway."

Poor guy.

Mya met her gaze. "Lir can handle them." She didn't doubt his abilities as a leader.

Jari threw her head back and laughed with that wide smile of hers. "Just let my man handle it. I know he can," she said in the girliest voice possible.

"Shut up." Mya pushed her, laughing.

Jari wrapped her arms around her shoulders. "Come on, let's go back to the table and relax a bit. That was intense."

They sat down at the table and downed another shot.

"I found myself a bad boy earlier and had a little rendezvous in the bathroom." Jari chuckled. "Did you see him?"

Mya had, and he certainly looked like a bad boy. One who needed a shower, but she didn't dare tell Jari that. "Yes, I saw him. More importantly, did the bartender see him?"

Jari winked one reptilian looking eye. "I do believe the bartender got an eye full. And an ear full."

"Good! Let him know what he passed up on. I hope he's stewing in jealousy."

Jari pulled her in and hugged her. "I love you!"

Growing up mostly alone and without anyone to call

family, Mya felt uncomfortable with the words *I love you.*
Instead of replying, she simply hugged her back. Tears welled
up in her eyes at the sentiment, though.

Finn and Mikail appeared at the table. Mikail looked
somewhat better already. Jari looked up with a smile and
clapped her hands.

"Who's up for a game of truth or dare?"

THEY ARRIVED AT HOME, sweaty, exhausted, and a little bit
drunk.

Mya *might* have had a little too much to drink. Jari had
convinced her to stay another hour after the encounter
between Alex and Mikail.

She found her way to Lir's room and started stripping off
her clothes, staggering as she did so. She came out of her
haze long enough to hear the sharp intake of breath from
somewhere in the room. Turning to look, she heard another
shocked gasp.

Lir was in his room, sitting on the bed.

Fuck. She snatched her dress—really just pieces of fabric
—and attempted to cover herself. "Sorry . . . I didn't
think . . . I thought you were in the living room," she
stuttered.

He struggled to relax his face as he tried to inconspicu-
ously cover the bulge in his pants. He stood to his full,
towering height. "It's ok. I should've told you I was in here or
something." He cleared his throat. "I just finished making the
bed for you, with some, uh, clean bedding."

Mya almost cried as she hugged him . . . while forgetting
she was naked. He backed up, pushing her body away from
his. And was that a tinge of red sweeping his collar?

"Maybe you should put some clothes on first, yeah?" He snatched one of his shirts from the dresser and handed it to her.

Grateful, she smiled and accepted the shirt. She threw the fabric over her head and, once again forgetting Lir was there, inhaled the scent of him embedded in the fibers. Salty ocean, mint, and tobacco. Everything was perfect until her gut tossed at the tobacco smell. She ran to the bathroom—as any lady would—and puked up the entire evening.

Lir stayed beside her, holding back her hair. No one had ever held her hair for her like that. She would've cried if not for the puking.

When she was sure she was done, she turned and smiled at him. "Thanks for taking care of me."

She stumbled to her feet, leaning against Lir as she took another step and almost fell. He scooped her up, carried her to the bed, and tucked her in. She nearly purred in approval.

He brushed her hair back from her face. "How much did you have to drink?" he asked in a soft voice.

She started doing drunken math in her head and laughed. "Lost count."

"Let me get you some crackers and water. A lot of water."

As Mya drifted into a fantasy of Lir doing more than getting her water, he came back and prodded her to open her eyes. She blinked them open as he shoved crackers into her mouth. There went the caring Lir. Now he was back to being annoyed and mean.

"Bloody hell, would you eat the fucking crackers?"

She struggled to sit up and then managed to eat them. She chugged some water down, and he made her swallow some aspirin.

She rested her head against the pillow and squinted at him. "Why didn't you go?"

"Go where? The club?"

She nodded, causing her head to throb. She instantly regretted the motion.

"I don't like to lose control, and nothing says loss of control like going to a club to party and get drunk."

"What's so wrong with losing control every once in a while? That's why you're so mean all the time, huh?"

He chuckled, surprising her. "Yeah, I suppose you have a point there, but I can't. If I lose control, I could miss an important call, and people could die. I can't risk it. It's too dangerous for everyone."

"That must really suck. I feel sorry for you, actually. Must be lonely and sad—" She stopped talking, catching on to the furrow of his brows and the tick in his jaw. "Never mind," she whispered, leaning her head back and closing her eyes with a sigh.

She felt him pull the covers over her body and kiss her forehead. She suppressed a smile at the kind gesture and rolled over, imagining his body wrapped around hers as she drifted off to sleep.

ैं

MYA WOKE UP, and the world felt . . . wrong. Like someone had taken a hammer to her head. The pain was excruciating. She raised her head.

Too dizzy. Ugh. What time is it?

With great effort, she pulled her phone off the charger. She didn't even remember getting into bed or charging her phone.

Three p.m.? Holy hell. I've slept all day!

Determined, she sat up and climbed out of bed. Every step was a forced effort. She would not be drinking herself into a hangover ever again. Wasn't that what people said? *I am never drinking again. This is the pits.* She stumbled to the bathroom to pee but stopped abruptly. She was wearing Lir's shirt!

Her memories flooded back. She'd taken off her clothes in front of him! How was she going to show her face now?

Fuck. My. Life!

She didn't want to take his shirt off, though, as she held it and inhaled his scent again. Maybe he wouldn't care? She ambled around and found some pajama pants, pulled them on, and headed out to the kitchen. She was starving.

She paused in the kitchen doorway, taking in the scene. The whole gang was awake. She'd been the only one still sleeping off her hangover.

Finn scraped eggs around on his plate, his skin green. Jari's head was plopped on the table. She was currently groaning. Alex clutched his stomach, hunched over. Lir reclined in his chair, his arms resting behind his head, apparently relaxing. Judging by the tick in his jaw, he was anything but relaxed. He was wound up like a spring top, ready to burst. Lir was pissed.

Without opening his eyes, he spoke. "Glad you could finally grace us with your presence." He said it with a growl.

She was still processing the room. "Um. I'm sorry? I didn't mean to sleep that long, your highness." She bowed with a sneer. She didn't want to deal with his moody ass while she was hungover. He could take his anger and shove it elsewhere.

He dropped his arms, ready to lunge, and stabbed her with his piercing blue eyes. They were the sea, flowing like an oceanic storm when he was angry. She could see the fire in them today, though. This was a special kind of anger.

Fuck me, she thought.

"Now that everyone is awake, maybe someone can explain to me why the mother fucking *Guardians* got drunk last night!" he yelled, projecting his words toward everyone in the room.

They collectively groaned at the explosive intrusion into their respective hangovers.

Mya chose to defend them. "Look, they were just having fun. Just trying to relax. And the place seemed safe enough."

Jari gave her a look and whispered, "Don't speak."

Lir looked positively vengeful as he turned his heated gaze back to Mya. "The place seemed *safe,* you say?" He stared at her for what felt like five minutes. "Tell me, why were you approached by Mikail? Hmm?"

"What does that have to do with anything?" She crossed her arms.

"He could have hurt you!" He threw his hands up in the air. "He's a fucking angel, and he has his sights on you. Do you have any idea what he could do to you? They"—he waved at the table of Guardians—"were supposed to be protecting you."

The Guardians' faces hung heavy with guilt.

"Instead, they got drunk and partied like a bunch of imbeciles. You never should've been taken to that club in the first place. I should've stopped this last night. I knew it was a bad idea!"

Mya was livid. How dare he treat her like a child! She might not have been as old as him, but she had been through too much for some asshole to try and control her again.

"Avalon is a place for supernatural beings, and I am a goddess. Why shouldn't I be able to go there?"

"A goddess? You're a useless one at that."

That fucking asshole. Who the hell does he think he is, calling me useless?

He'd found the one insult that would hurt, and he'd used it against her. It hurt more because it was true. And because it came from him.

"Excuse me?" she choked out, struggling to hold back the tears.

"Hell, I'm sor—"

"You have no right. *None!* You don't know me!"

"I didn't mean to hurt—"

"Fuck you! Get off your high horse, you arrogant asshole. You don't get to tell everyone what to do just because you think you're better than us." Her chest rose and fell with her heavy breaths as a powerful feeling stirred within her.

"Christ, woman. Can't you accept my fucking apology?" He asked it as if it were a reasonable request. "No, you have to rant about how I think I'm better than you. Please, I am trying to protect you!"

"Protect me? More like judge me. That's all you do! Boss everyone around and judge people."

"Is that the best you got, sweetheart? I'm bossy and judgmental?" He was laughing at her now. He pulled out a cigarette, lit it, and let the smoke out on an exhale. "Come on, say it. Call me a bastard. An asshole with a smoking problem. Every fucking word is true." He raised his arms. "Come on, hit me, baby. You wanna do it. You know you do."

He was mad at himself, she realized. That was the real reason he was so pissed. He hadn't been there to protect her and keep her safe, and he was taking his anger out on them because he was . . . afraid for her?

"You know what? I'm not going to help you beat yourself up. Just accept that we all made mistakes last night and move on." She turned away and ran to his room, slamming the bedroom door behind her. It felt good.

"That's nice. Run and hide. In my own fucking room, I'll remind you!" he yelled through the door.

Ignoring him, Mya ran to the bathroom, stripped off his shirt, and considered ripping it to shreds. She stepped into the heated embrace of the shower, letting the hot water run over her sore muscles. After some time under the steaming, pounding pressure, she cried. She vented out her frustration with Lir.

She glanced up from her despair and spotted his bottle of Head & Shoulders shampoo. A mischievous idea flitted through her mind. She smiled at her own brilliance. This would require patience. It could be weeks from now, but she wouldn't forget her anger. Even if she had maybe, sort of forgiven him already.

Feeling better, she climbed out of the shower and dressed. She heard a soft knock on the door.

"It's me. Can I come in?" Jari asked softly.

Mya opened the door, and Jari cringed.

"You look like hell," she said.

"Thanks. I feel like hell."

"I'm sorry. We should've gone home when you wanted to."

Mya chuckled. "It's ok. I had fun. Eventually."

Jari laughed. "You did? I can't believe you kissed that angel, though."

"I did *what?*" Mya's eyes went wide.

"You don't remember?"

"No."

Jari gave her a sympathetic smile. "Well, if it helps, Alex dared you to."

Of fucking course. Mya had trouble backing down from a dare. "I'm going to kick his ass for that."

"Don't worry. We'll beat him up together."

Jari was turning out to be the best friend she'd ever had since that two-timer she refused to think about.

Mya held out her hand. "Pinky promise?"

Jari paused, then wrapped her pinky around hers. "Pinky promise."

They both laughed then.

"Hey, I'm sorry about Lir." Jari said softly. "He means well, but he can be a major jackass sometimes." She wiggled her brow. "Plus, I think Alex told him about your kiss with our little seraphim."

Shit. "Of course he did. Now, we really need to kick his ass. It's ok, though. I'll get over it," Mya lied. She was mortified.

"If it makes you feel better, I'm pretty sure Lir is in the kitchen making you an apology cake."

It did make her feel better. "Good. It better taste delicious."

Jari looked around the room. "Did you snoop around yet?" She cocked a grin.

Mya slipped into her best southern accent. "Why no, I didn't."

They shared a glance before they jumped out of bed and started snooping.

Lir's room was surprisingly feminine. White and light-blue bed linens covered his large Cali-king bed. The frame was a light oaken color. His pretty, white nightstand and dresser belonged in a magazine. Light, gauzy curtains framed the windows, and the French doors offered a perfect view of the sea lying just outside. Mya understood why he chose this room. It was so close to home, he couldn't resist.

After several minutes of looking, Mya determined Lir was a veritable saint. She found nothing but clothes, seashells, weapons, and books. Other than that, his room was a blank canvas. He didn't even have pictures.

Resigned, both she and Jari flopped back on the bed, side by side.

"Let's watch TV," Jari suggested.

"Let's!" She grinned with her response.

They settled on some trash TV, and Mya eventually drifted off to sleep, still feeling hungover.

While she slept, the goddess of Nyx visited her and decided to show her a vision of her past.

CHAPTER FOURTEEN

NYX

Nyx rested on a bed of feathers in the underworld, drenched in sweat, despite the cold, dreary cave she lay in. Distantly, she heard the drip of water from the stalactites, though she couldn't see them in the darkness. She didn't mind the dark. Darkness was her salvation. She lived in the shadows. Her husband, Erebus, was darkness himself.

No, she did not mind it at all.

Though she didn't love Erebus. Not one bit. He was her brother and had forced her to bear his child, all for more power. She shoved down the painful memories of being raped by him. If she let them out, they would torment her.

She hated how everyone claimed she and Erebus were in love, oblivious to the scars she bore. The scars so many women bore. Men could be such selfish bastards.

An unbearable pain ripped through her abdomen. She was giving birth to their first-born child, and had she known of the agony that came with it, she would've sworn off children entirely before undertaking this endeavor. She had been sweating, pushing, and screaming for hours. She didn't know for how many, only that the moon had risen and fallen in all of that time.

Oh, how she longed for the moon to rise again. She could pull some of that power and use it. Another wave of agony crashed through her. Unable to prevent it, she screamed through the pain. How much longer could this be? She couldn't take it. She wanted to die, if only to remove the pain.

Her sister, Gaia, kneeled between her legs. "Almost there, Nyx. I can see the babe's head." Gaia placed a comforting hand on her thigh. "Come on, one more push."

Nyx wailed. "No. I cannot bear it."

Gaia pressed on. "Yes, you can. You can do this. Every mother can give birth. It is our natural power."

Nyx felt that dreadful wave rise up once again and knew she had to push with everything she had. She screamed and screamed and bore down. Finally, she felt some semblance of relief and heard the blessed crying of a newborn babe.

"She is healthy and alive, Nyx," Gaia cooed. "You should feel blessed!" Her sister wrapped the baby in a black sheet of silk and handed her over.

Nyx marveled at her beauty. Her baby, her shining star, for she shone brighter than the sun itself, lighting up the cave and chasing away the darkness. She was brilliant.

Nyx was in love.

For the first time in her life, she felt love. She watched as the newborn babe suckled her breast and cooed to her. She knew at that moment she would protect this precious little one for all eternity. This child was hers; nothing and no one would change that.

The vision was ripped away from Mya with parting words from Nyx, her voice full of sorrow. "My daughter, Aether. The one who killed me."

❧

MYA

Mya woke up with a start, sweating as if she'd undergone childbirth herself. She could still feel faint remnants of the pain, and silently cursed Nyx for giving her that vision. She didn't want to know about her past life. She wasn't Nyx. She was Mya, damn it, and she just wanted to feel normal. She didn't want to feel like a goddess. Didn't want the pain and grief of losing the love from your own child. It was horrible.

She lay down again and struggled to fall back asleep, silently afraid of the things Nyx would show her.

Shortly after falling asleep, Mya woke with a start for the second time that night, covered in sweat. As she lay in bed, she looked into the dark eyes staring down at her. They were accompanied by a sinful smile.

Alex.

She tried to push him away and failed. It was like trying to move a mountain. She sighed. "What do you want, Alex?"

"Training day." He grinned even wider.

"What the hell do you mean?"

He gave her a nefarious look, backed up, and said, "The boss wants you to learn how to fight, and since I'm the best, I get to train you."

She spotted the bag lying next to him, filled with various weapons. That was a little exciting, but she wasn't climbing out of bed for anything.

"Why do I need to wake up now? The sun's not even up. Can't we train later?" She hated how whiny she sounded, but she didn't care. She was exhausted.

Alex strolled over to the window and flung open the curtains. The sun blared in.

"One, I'm bored," he said. "Two, if I can't sleep in, you can't sleep in. And three, your enemy won't wait for you to be well-rested before he attacks. You must learn to be ready to fight in any situation."

She hated that he made sense.

"He? Are you implying that all my enemies will be males, or that I don't need to be ready to fight women?" She was grasping.

He saw right through her charade and snorted. "You knew what I meant. Besides, women don't bring the battle to your doorstep. They fight vindictively, preferring poison and sneaky warfare. Worse, you never know when a woman will attack. It could be today, tomorrow, or ten years from now. If you want my true opinion, I think women are better at war."

She didn't expect that conclusion. She couldn't come up with anything to say to it. Alex actually respected women— or somewhat did. Or maybe he just thought they were better at war, as he stated. Either way, she would take the compliment.

He paused, furrowing one scarred brow. "Get out of bed, woman. Weakness will not be tolerated!"

Ok, she mused, *there goes the respect idea.*

"Fine," she grumbled, and climbed out of bed. "Can I shower first?"

He looked at her as if she had suggested he slip into a tutu and parade through Times Square. "Why in all the realms would you need to shower when you're about to train and get dirty? Do you think your enemy cares if you shower?" he said, as if he knew she wasn't listening.

She had a feeling she would be subjected to a lot of these "your enemy" talks.

She concealed her laughter with a cough. "Sorry. I'll just get dressed."

Alex stared down at her, lingering on her legs again before lifting his eyes and stopping at her chest. She crossed her arms in indignation.

"Is that Lir's shirt?" he asked, his tone now more serious than the act of disemboweling enemies.

"No," she lied.

"Uh-huh."

"Am I allowed to eat at least?" Her stomach grumbled in response.

"I will allow it . . . for now."

"Gee, thank you, your majesty."

"Next smart-ass comment will earn you push-ups. Your stringy arms need them. Hold back the tongue. Got it?"

She fucking hated push-ups.

Alex leveled a look at her that would set forests on fire. She got ready in record time.

❦

MYA WAS FALLING AGAIN through a spinning tunnel of blackness. She hated portal travel more than anything she had yet done in her life. She tried to remember to relax and pay attention to her feet. She was so tired of looking like a fool by falling every time she exited the portal. The ground came tumbling toward her, all too fast, as it did every single time. She bent her knees slightly, felt for the ground, and still fell.

"Aargh!"

Alex landed like a cat—light on his feet—and laughed. "Still aren't used to the portal, huh?"

She grumbled but held back the rude comment on the tip of her tongue, if only to save her poor arms from the promised push-ups.

Around her, insects chirped, birds sang, and animals rummaged. They were in the forest.

Please, no.

She hated the outdoors, bugs, sun, and nature. The more she thought about it, the more her skin began to itch. She looked around, taking in her new hell. Trees lined everything as far as she could see, each one easily over one hundred feet tall as it towered into the sky. The further out she looked, the denser the trees packed together, providing a thick canopy of shade. The sun barely peeked through, yet she could still feel the sticky, humid heat of the day.

She breathed in the fresh air. She did enjoy the scent of pine trees. "Why are we in the forest?"

Alex whipped out a knife and started cutting through branches. "The forest is an excellent landscape for training. We'll hike to a location, and from there, we'll train with weapons." He kept going, not really talking to Mya as much as just talking. "The hike will help you hone your endurance while the woodsy ground will help you with your balance and agility." He sounded like a dojo master. He probably didn't even know what that was.

An hour, an eternity maybe—she didn't know—had passed as they walked to the training spot. She had a feeling Alex didn't really have a particular spot in mind and was just pushing her. Her legs burned, screaming at her to stop using them. Her chest heaved, lungs flaming, throat dry. She stumbled over yet another branch, marring her skin with even more scratches. She tumbled to the ground.

"Ow!" she groaned, and used a tree to pull herself back to her feet. She brushed twigs out of her hair, leaning on the tree as she tried to catch her breath. "Tell me you brought water at least?"

He snorted. "Nope. Survival means you find your own water."

She dropped her arms in protest. "You're trying to kill me!"

"Nah, you're a goddess. You won't die from something as simple as dehydration."

That was reassuring . . . almost.

"How do we find water, then, o wise one?"

The joke went over his head. "Listen. Try to hear the water. Smell. Try to sniff out the moisture in the air. Watch. Follow the animals. They'll be near the water."

She was surprised he didn't spout off some bullshit about being one with nature after a speech like that. She couldn't hear the water, but there had been animals nearby, and the air had been humid for the duration of their hike. Had they been near the water since they got here? She tried to tap into her "goddess senses" and found it was pretty damn hard. Busy honing her abilities, her foot sank into a puddle of squishy mud.

"Water!" The earth made a sucking sound as she pulled her foot from the ground. She didn't even care that it was now caked in dirt. She'd done it. She'd found water!

She followed the liquid on the ground, parted a branch from in front of her face, and stared at the most beautiful body of water she'd ever seen—though it was really nothing more than a small, bubbling stream. She stepped across the wet pebbles and leaned over the water, scooping some into her hands and drinking from it.

"Took you long enough," Alex said, voice dripping with sarcasm.

"Hey, I'm learning here."

He paused and crossed his arms over his chest. "Push-ups! Now! Let's go!"

She grumbled to herself and accomplished one push-up before her arms refused to do another.

"That is the most pathetic thing I have ever seen."

"It's my first day, Alex!"

"I was born with the ability to do a hundred push-ups or more."

Well, duh. "You're the god of war!" she yelled. "How were you born, though? Enlighten a curious woman, would ya?"

He cocked his head and shrugged. "I have parents. I was a child, once. I think." That was all he said.

She racked her mind for those distant Greek mythology lessons from high school, searching for anything about the god of war. She was pretty sure he was Ares.

"Are your parents really Zeus and Hera?"

His casual demeanor ceased as he shot her a look. His eyes blazed with fire that belonged in the pits of hell. "Yes, and that's all I'll tell you, so cease your questions immediately."

"Sorry," she mumbled.

His stiffened posture relaxed a little, though his eyes still blazed. "I forget you were raised like a human and must have some human mannerisms. How many push-ups can humans do when they're born?"

She laughed. Was he so out of touch? "None."

He frowned. "That explains some things." He let out a long sigh. "You were raised with this weak human mentality."

She wasn't sure how to explain to a god that humans were born as babies with underdeveloped muscles and couldn't even lift their heads at first. She could just imagine Alex's shocked facial expression at that one and decided it was best to let the topic go. Instead, she focused on quenching her thirst and relieving the dry ache in her throat.

"Hurry up. You're far too slow." He tapped his foot impatiently.

She grumbled and cursed him under her breath. After scooping up one more drink of water, she stood, ready again to walk for an ungodly number of hours. She peeled off some strips of fabric from her shirt. She would have to mark some trees and hope she could find water again. She thought Alex would be proud.

Though, maybe not.

CHAPTER FIFTEEN

MYA

They arrived at a small clearing in a dense section of trees, and Alex declared they would stop there. She scuttled off to find some privacy. Her bladder had been yelling at her for forever now, and she couldn't wait to pee.

"Gods do not need to pee so often," Alex called after her.

She didn't care what Alex thought of her bladder. She had a feeling she was about to be subjected to a long day of "gods don't do that."

Relieved, she headed back to the clearing, massaging her legs on the way. They burned something fierce. Alex had placed numerous guns on the ground. He pulled out the accompanying bullets.

His gaze moved from the gun in his hand to her. "Since you're weak, we'll start with guns."

She glossed over the insult and focused on the part that made her giddy. She could handle guns. She'd learned how to shoot and had even obtained a conceal and carry permit after leaving her asshole ex-boyfriend.

She bent over to examine the guns before noticing Hecate watching them, seated in a recliner with her legs propped up.

How the hell did she get a recliner here? And is that a cold Coke? Her mouth watered as the desire for that sweet soda surged inside her. She had a momentary image of strangling Hecate as she drained her Coke, only for the image to be replaced by one where she lunged to attack, and Hecate blasted her away with a mere wave of her hand. Knowing the second image was more realistic, she tried to ignore the icy-cold glass of refreshment.

She motioned toward the goddess of magic. "What's she doing here?"

He shrugged his massive shoulders. The sun glinted off his tattoo, and it almost looked like the damn thing was moving again. "She likes to follow me."

Mya looked to Hecate for confirmation. She had a feeling Hecate wouldn't like that comment.

The sorceress spoke up. "I wanted to see the god of war in action. That's all." She then saluted Mya with her cold Coke. "Good luck, Mya."

On second thought, maybe she would attempt to strangle Hecate after all.

Alex handed her a small handgun. "We'll start simple. This is a Taurus," he said as he took out the magazine. "These are called 9mm bullets." He reinserted the magazine, pulled back the slide, and turned the gun on its side. "The safety is on." He pushed the button down. "Now it's off." He was giving her the guns-for-children talk.

She silently laughed at him.

He pointed to a target pinned to a tree, then raised the gun and fired as if it were an extension of his own hand. The way he moved took her breath away. Bullets flew at the target faster than she'd ever seen. She didn't know a gun could even shoot at those speeds.

He turned toward her, and a smile lit up his face. "You can close your mouth now, little goddess. Your turn."

She sputtered and realized, with horror, that her mouth was indeed open.

He handed the gun to her. She got into her stance, supported the weapon the way she'd been taught, and took a deep breath. She narrowed her focus and fired. She wasn't as fast as Alex, but she was competent enough. Emptying the clip, she turned to face him.

He raised his brows just a fraction. "Not bad, just work on your speed. When did you learn to shoot?"

She shrugged to prove his compliment hadn't fazed her, though secretly, she loved it. "My ex-boyfriend was abusive, and it took me a long time to leave him. Afterwards, I needed protection."

Alex stepped closer to her, his eyes burning with fierce anger. "Did he hurt you?"

Mya shrugged as if she didn't care, but her voice broke from the emotion. "He did." She cleared her throat. "When I finally got the courage to leave, I spent weeks looking over my shoulder. I decided it was time to protect myself and started going to the gun range. Eventually, the instructor took notice and started teaching me how to shoot."

Alex wore a sympathetic look, and she hated it. She didn't want people to feel sorry for her. She wanted people to look at her, hear her story and say, "Hey, you did the right thing. You should be proud of yourself."

Alex seemed to catch on to her reluctance to talk about the subject any longer and gestured to the guns on the ground. "What else can you shoot?"

She rattled off what she'd learned to use. "Some shot-guns, 9 mm, .22 handguns, a .45, and an AR-15."

"Ok then." He picked up an AK-47. "What about this?"

She was all but jumping in excitement. "Never shot that."

He handed her the gun, and she stroked it lovingly.

"Come to mama."

Alex chuckled a bit as he ran her through the operating basics, safety, and stance. Finally ready, she started shooting. The gun was a beast. The bullets spewed out in a fast *rat-a-tat-tat,* every motion smooth with barely any recoil. Though, the slight pushing against her shoulder eventually caused it to ache. With the clip emptied, she felt satisfied. Handing the gun back to Alex, she watched as he also stroked it with love.

He looked up at her, his eyes sparkling. "Want to see something cool?" he asked.

She nodded with a grin.

"Watch this." He lifted the AK and started shooting, even though the clip was empty. The gun transformed into a variety of ten different guns before he was done.

"What?" she shrieked. "How?"

"That was first-hand experience of the god of war powers. I can turn any weapon into another weapon, and I never need to reload."

"Any weapon?"

"Yep."

"Knives?"

"Yes."

She paused and smiled. "Flame-thrower?"

His tone became short. "Yes."

"Ax?"

He glared at her. "I said *any weapon!"*

"Sorry, just trying to wrap my head around your bad-ass

powers." She decided a compliment would help, and his powers *were* pretty badass.

He smirked at that but said nothing.

Mya turned toward the other goddess. "Hey, did Hecate see that?"

Hecate was still reclining in the armchair. Her spirit forms had arrived at some point, and they waved handheld fans to keep her cool.

Hecate stared at Alex with an obvious interest in her eyes. "Yes, dear. I saw his display of power."

"She totally wants you," Mya whispered to Alex.

He scoffed. "I don't mess with witches. Too dangerous."

"Oh, the god of war is scared of a little witch?" Mya teased.

"You bet your sweet ass I am," he said with laughter in his voice.

"Best not let Hecate know that, especially if she wants to sleep with you. She might curse you"—she glanced down to the juncture between his thighs—"with some performance issues." Mya was giggling now.

Alex covered his groin protectively as if Hecate really would curse him. The concept wasn't that far off, considering all the things they'd seen the sorceress do so far. Who knew how vast her powers truly were?

"Now we need to build up your strength," Alex said, changing the topic of conversation. He walked her through some stretches before making her do sit-ups, lift weights, and perform the gods-awful push-ups. After some time, he changed things up. "Now, we work on your running."

She clutched her chest, breathing hard. She would keel over and die if she had to endure much more of his training. "You can't be serious."

He leaned down to look her in the eyes. "As a heart attack. Let's go. I'd like to be home before nightfall."

She leaned her head back in exasperation. "We've been doing this all day!"

"Yep." He bent to pick up his weapons.

"And you still want me to run?"

"Yep."

"I hate you."

He laughed at her. "Yeah, yeah. I know. Hurry up!" He smacked her ass, causing her to yelp.

She ran, ran, and ran some more as Alex followed her, barking out insults of encouragement. When she couldn't push her body anymore, she fell on the ground in fatigue for the tenth time. He finally declared they were done and conjured up a portal to take them home. She didn't even care when the portal dropped her on her ass again.

She landed in the backyard of the safe house, lifted her head from the grass, and looked toward the house with longing. "Just gotta move a little more," she pleaded to herself.

Finn stood from where he was crouched over a planter—playing with his plants, she assumed. Her eyes took in the ruffled hot-pink garden apron, and she laughed.

"Nice apron!"

Finn chuckled, and his green eyes appeared to almost glow. "I happen to love pink, and the pockets are awesome." He took out a handful of gardening tools, then shoved them in all the pockets to show her before heading her way.

She lifted a brow. "You just happen to love pink?"

Finn winked, plucked her from the ground, dusted off her clothes, and set her on wobbly legs. He took in her disheveled hair, banged up knees, and the mud that seemed to be all over her body. "What happened to you?"

"Alex is training me." She threw up air quotes over the last bit.

Finn looked at the god of war with a sparkle in his eye. "Aww, did Alexander the Great train you too hard?"

"I told you not to call me that!"

"Freedom of speech. Look it up." Finn winked at her.

Alex flipped him off and headed to the house, the sun highlighting the sparkling sweat on his skin. She tried not to notice.

Finn looked down at Mya with a smile. "Want me to kick his ass?"

"No, that's okay."

Finn nudged her shoulder. "Watch this."

He opened his palm, and Mya watched in amazement as his skin turned green and a vine slithered out of his finger. It continued to grow until a single bud appeared. Ebony petals fell into place, forming a single black rose. Finn handed her the flower with a flirty look in his eye. It was a beautiful gesture and almost made up for the grueling day she'd had.

"Thanks, Finn. I love it!" She meant every word.

Lir appeared in the doorway, his raven hair tousled and his black button up shirt slightly undone. In an effort to ignore his delicious body and halt her lusty desires, she reminded herself that he was the one who'd wanted her trained. She would hate him right along with Alex.

"Just in time. We've got a Guardian call. Let's go." He looked Mya over. "You should stay here and bathe."

She huffed and crossed her arms. "Thanks for clearing that up for me. I wasn't quite sure I needed one," she called out, but Lir had already disappeared into the house.

Ugh! That man is infuriating.

Without another word, she trudged to Lir's bedroom where an extra-large bathtub called to her.

"Hey, you track mud in my bathroom, you clean it," Lir said.

"Bite me," she snapped back, and slammed the door before he could respond to her.

She placed the rose on the dresser and headed to the bathroom, ignoring the mirror. The sight would be quite terrifying. She stripped off her clothes as the bathtub filled. Once the water was hot enough, she stepped in with a sigh.

She soaked in the tub, feeling a bit depressed as the heat slowly relaxed her sore muscles. How could she be a goddess? She still felt like a human. She could barely move out there, while Alex had no trouble at all. Hell, he wasn't even that dirty. Meanwhile, *she* looked like roadkill. Maybe she would feel better after they were able to release her powers, but at that moment, she wanted to go back to being a poor, human waitress.

That thought depressed her even more.

Fuck this miserable attitude, she thought as she climbed out of the tub, dried off, and slipped into bed. She was beyond tired, and at least she couldn't pout in her sleep. Plus, her body definitely needed some rest.

⚜

HECATE

HECATE HAD WATCHED Mya and Alex as they trained. They shared an agreeable companionship that she envied. When had she ever had a friend like that? Hecate had always been alone. Even gods kept their distance from someone who controlled magic. Alex was a perfect example. Hecate had always been ostracized by someone or another.

Which was why she made a promise to herself long ago

that she would never show weakness. She made it a point to always appear strong, independent, and valuable. If they didn't want *her*, she would make them want her skills and magic.

"Like Alex," a small voice whispered to herself.

Gods, she envied his strength. Alex thought he was less than the god he once was, which was why he'd renamed himself. Perhaps he'd changed over the centuries, but she knew he was still the formidable warrior she'd seen in battle so long ago. She could see his powerful aura, blazing with a red glow of strength. She watched as he handled his gun with ease. She let her gaze roam along his strong shoulders, his fierce tattoo. Not weak at all.

What would it feel like to run her tongue along his torso, feel his powerful hands stroking her, his long fingers . . . ?

She sank into a fantasy of the two of them leaning against a tree as he used his massive arms to hold her up, pumping into her with a savage fierceness.

Oh no! No, no, no! she scolded herself. *One must not think of Alex that way!* She loved his strength, yes. She would admit that to herself. And yes, he was beyond sexy. But she would not sleep with that vile being under any circumstances. He hated her with a passion that was wholly unfair and undeserved. She came here to help them, yet he treated her like she had some unforgivable agenda!

Although, it was true. She wasn't here out of the goodness of her own heart. No, she was here because she was becoming horribly weak.

She hated admitting that to herself. She hated how all those humans had made her vulnerable as they turned their backs on magic. She hated that she needed the arrogant Guardians for protection. She hated everyone and everything!

She was so angry. Gods, she was so angry. She wanted to

go back to a time when she was the all-mighty and all-powerful witch she once was. She covertly conserved her magic now, never letting anyone know her secret. Always pretending. Always wearing her mask of armor, her mask of indifference.

She was tired of pretending. She didn't want to need Alex and his strength. She wanted to be stronger than him, not *pretend* that she was. Then she could laugh in his face for hating her so much and give him a reason to hate her!

She drifted off into another fantasy of Alex, this one of violence.

Yes, much better.

She closed her eyes and drifted off to sleep in the afternoon sun. Her spirits would watch over her.

CHAPTER SIXTEEN

LIR

Lir snuck into his room. Mya was already asleep, and he didn't want to disturb her. He should've gathered his gear already, but got caught up in all his Guardian prep crap. Time always seemed to get away from him. He pulled on his battle gear—leather pants, a leather jacket, and gnarly shit-kicker boots.

He didn't bother with being discreet. Mya was snoring now. Nothing would wake her at this point. As he looked at her small, very feminine figure, he found he was worried about her. Too much, perhaps, but if they were to use her in the war, she had a long way to go.

She had lived her entire life as a human, therefore, she was weak like one. He remembered their earlier fight. Having known she felt upset and useless, he shouldn't have said those things to her. It was just that she made his blood boil, and sometimes he couldn't help but lash out. No one had ever raised that kind of reaction in him before.

He was known to be an angry and stressed guy, but he

was level-headed in addressing issues. He knew when to say certain things and when to hold back on others that were too harmful. What made Mya different? And why did she grip his interest in an iron-clad hold? He couldn't stop staring at her as she lay there in a restful sleep.

The buzz of his phone snapped him out of his mental fog. He ignored it. He hated cell phones and didn't understand how to use them. Gathering up his weapons, he headed out to battle.

Battle he understood . . . so much more than women and cellphones.

☙❧

Lir surveyed the crowded shopping mall. Shoppers filled the area, screaming and falling on top of one another. He shook his head as one man shoved someone over the banister in his haste to get away.

Survival of the fittest, he mused.

No one cared who they injured as they scrambled away from the monsters. It was complete pandemonium, and it had Zeus written all over it.

What's that arrogant fool up to now?

Alex pulled his sword from its sheath. "Vrykolakas," he growled.

"The bloody, fecking bastard is using Vrykolakas," Finn said at the same time.

Vrykolakas were undead werewolves under Zeus's control. Lir recalled what he knew about the monsters—the truth, not the doctored version which had been altered by eons of history and stories. He hadn't seen them in centuries and had even thought them extinct. He knew better now.

A long time ago, Zeus—doing what he did best—slept

with a woman he shouldn't have. The woman's father, Lycaon, challenged Zeus. The god retaliated by cursing the man and his entire family to become werewolves. When those werewolves died, they became the Vrykolakas, which must answer to only Zeus. They also happened to feed off human blood and flesh.

What made the creatures even deadlier was their human appearance. They had deceptive, milky skin, gray eyes, and flaming red hair. They didn't appear as monsters until it was too late. By the time they opened their mouths to reveal rows of fangs, their victim was already dead.

If Zeus released them on the humans like this, he was declaring war.

"You know what to do!" Lir instructed the Guardians. He had to yell to be heard over the growing screams. He raised his sword and gave it a couple of test swings. They would all need to perform at their highest caliber for this battle. He gave his last command. "Do not falter. Do not hesitate. One wrong move could be the difference between life and death." Lir grimaced, remembering the many bloody battles where Vrykolakas were involved.

The carnage was a thing he wouldn't soon forget.

"Aye!" Finn pulled out his second battle-axe. He normally only used one.

Lir considered pulling a second weapon himself, but decided against it. His mastery with a single sword would be of better benefit to this fight. He wouldn't underestimate the Vrykolakas, though. That was the quickest way to get yourself killed.

Jari unsheathed her dual katanas, twirling them in the air. "Got it, boss." Her smile had a slightly deranged tilt. "Let's get bloody, boys." She always had a thirst for blood.

They all did.

"We need to get the humans to safety," Lir said as he looked for an exit.

The humans were still screaming, running, and pushing each other in their panic.

He spotted an exit and saw that the human cops were now on the scene. "Damn it all to hell! The cops are here!"

"Ah, fuck. Now we must protect them while they try to be heroes," Alex said, annoyed.

Lir directed the Guardians to usher the humans out while he approached the cops, hoping to talk some sense into them. The officers recoiled at the sight of him. Some of their faces paled, and he spotted one discreetly covering his pants. They lifted their guns toward him as one unit. It was almost impressive. They weren't all cowards, just the one who'd peed his pants.

Lir held up his arms in surrender but didn't dare drop his sword. With the monsters prowling at his back, that would have been suicide. He wasn't afraid of the little mortal cops, anyway.

"I'm not here to harm you," he said in his most commanding tone. "My name is Lir. I am a Guardian, and I am here to protect you. You're dealing with monsters down there that you aren't prepared for, and it's not safe for you. You're no match for those creatures. You must leave."

They looked around at each other, not sure what to do.

"Why should we?" a middle-aged, overweight cop asked, pointing his finger at Lir with his lips pressed tight.

Lir didn't understand why the humans accepted unhealthy men to protect them. Surely they should have better standards.

"Because you will die," he said plainly, looking into each officer's eyes as he spoke. "The monsters will murder all of you. They'll feast on your dead body, and it will happen so fast, you won't even know they've done it."

One of the cops snorted. "Uh-huh, and we're supposed to believe the crazy guy holding a sword? Where'd you even get that thing? eBay?"

All the cops laughed.

What the hell is eBay? These fools were the ones talking nonsense. The arrogant cops had exhausted his patience. "You know what? Go ahead and die. Don't say I didn't warn you." He gave them his back, knowing if they shot him, the bullets would bounce right off and give the cops an eyeful. He laughed inwardly, wishing he had time to turn around and see their faces.

Sure enough, the sound of gunfire echoed through the air. No doubt the guns had gained the attention of the Vrykolakas.

"Jesus, Mary, and Joseph!" a cop shouted behind him.

Lir ignored him and continued walking toward the massacre. When he reached the marble banister, he launched his body over it, landing in an agile crouch. The smooth marble cracked beneath him on impact.

Oops.

A Vrykolaka greeted him with a mouthful of fangs. He responded with a sword through its neck. Its head slid off in one smooth motion. Knowing the monster wasn't yet dead, he chopped off the limbs, then cut those in half again.

Messy work. Blood drenched him after only one kill. Another creature landed on his back and sunk its fangs into his neck. Pain lanced through him.

Motherfucker.

He tried to buck it off and failed. The creature was too strong. He summoned his power and let the water wrap around his body in a swirling tempest. The Vrykolaka lost its grip and began slipping. Lir spun on his heel and thrust his sword into the monster's gut. The intestines spilled out over the marble. The Vrykolaka wasn't the least bit fazed and continued to move around, trying to latch onto his body again. Lir shifted his sword, following the creature's wild movements. He was barely scratching it. The Vrykolaka, growing impatient, screamed in his face, spitting all over him.

"Was that really necessary?" He smirked.

The creature, failing to understand his humor, screamed again, assaulting Lir with the smell of blood and dead flesh. Had he been a weaker god, he would've puked his guts up right then and there.

Instead, he used all his strength and clipped the Vrykolaka with an uppercut to the jaw. The sound of cracking bone split the air. Without hesitation, he kicked out a crushing blow to the monster's ribs and was rewarded with another splintering sound.

The creature hunched over, clutching its torso. Lir used that moment to raise his sword and deliver a final strike. He found his target, and the head slid off in slow motion. He kicked it away and hacked the rest of the carcass up as fast as he could.

Two down.

He looked around and spotted about ten more.

Finn battled two of them. Every step, pure brute force. Headbutting, kicking, and even biting. He spun both his axes through the air and hacked the Vrykolakas into pieces. Next, he conjured up a couple rose vines from his hands. They wrapped around the creature's head, squeezing until it popped off with a sickening squelch.

Two more Vrykolakas descended on Lir as he watched Finn's battle.

Damn it!

He'd become distracted. One landed on his back, and the

other jumped in front of him. He swung his sword, staving off the one at his front. He was moving the weapon too wildly for his comfort. Lir preferred perfection at all times. He called upon the sea once more and embraced the water wrapping around his body. The creature on his back slipped and slid, but did not lose its grip. Using his legs for leverage, Lir performed a backflip and smashed the Vrykolaka into the ground. The force caused the marble to crack further, and the ground split in two, taking the Vrykolaka down with it. He'd worry about that one later.

He turned back toward the one in front and shot his hand out. Water swirled around the creature, cutting off its air supply as it scratched at its neck. Lir suppressed a smile. Nothing would move that water but him. With the creature busy drowning, he swung his blade, slicing off its head. With a few quick slices, he hacked it up.

Two more attacked him. He kicked out and hit one square in the chest while swinging his sword around and removing a hand from another. Blood sprayed all around him. He used the momentum to swing the sword in the direction of the Vrykolaka at his front and guided the blade into its neck. That head fell to the ground as well. Adrenaline fueled him as he hacked both bodies into pieces.

He turned his attention to the rest of the battle again, ensuring he didn't get distracted once more. Alex, Finn, and Jari were finishing off their kills.

Just as he thought the battle was ending, the creature that had fallen into the crack crawled out of it, snarling and hissing as it wrapped a gnarly hand around his ankle. Wasting no time, Lir raised his sword and sliced off its hand. Then he swung down, and the sword stabbed into the top of its head, splitting its flesh in two. The blade slowed, stopping at its jaw.

"That's disgusting. Sorry about that." Lir yanked out the sword, blood and brain matter clinging to the blade. He shook the gore away and hacked at the body until he was sure the Vrykolaka was dead.

He could feel the poison coursing through his veins from the bite he'd taken. It wouldn't kill him, but he would definitely be out of commission for a bit after this.

Alex looked up at him. Blood covered him, and he still held the arm he'd just amputated from a dead body. "You all right, boss?"

Lir's breathing was labored as he spoke. "For now." He addressed the group, making sure his voice didn't waver despite his shallow breath. "They all dead?"

"Yep," they said in unison.

"Casualties?" That was all he could say at that point.

"A few dumbass cops decided to join the fight and died," Jari said. "A dozen humans. The rest escaped."

Not too horrible. He had expected as much. "Alright. Can you finish up and burn them?"

"Yep," Jari replied.

Finn nodded. Alex was busy chopping up more bodies.

Using the last of his energy, Lir created a portal home. Stumbling, he trudged to his bedroom, dropping his weapons along the way. He didn't care where they landed. He had to shower, just wash the blood off. He needed to get through this last task, and then he could sleep. Blessed sleep.

Fumbling with the handle, he turned on the shower and stripped off his clothes. Every step was pure agony. He could feel the Vrykolaka's poison infecting his body, like fire spreading through his veins. It burned so fierce, he could barely move his legs. With a shaking hand, he scrubbed his skin, only to fall into the glass door as the weakness set in. He grabbed onto the tile, trying to pull himself up, but his hands slipped, and he fell back onto the floor of the shower stall.

"Come on, you weak son of bitch, get up!" he yelled at himself.

Mya entered the bathroom, turning eyes as big as saucers his way. "Lir? Are you ok?"

He struggled to respond, his voice coming out in a whisper. "Yeah, just . . . weak."

Without hesitation, she reached into the shower and heaved him up onto the inner bench. She stepped in and washed his body with precise movements, averting her gaze to avoid the whole "you're naked, and this is awkward" bit. He needed help, and she didn't want him to turn her away.

Lir felt grateful for his fall, which caused Mya to wake up and help him. That concerned him. He was independent to a fault; his pride always got the best of him. He preferred to be the one who helped, but never the one who accepted it.

Mya turned off the water and snagged a towel. She dried him efficiently, every movement professional. And to think, he'd called her useless and weak.

I'm such an asshole.

"Thank you, Mya." He struggled to get the words out. "I mean it. This means a lot to me."

She blinked in surprise and stared at him for a long moment. "Are you dying?"

He would have chuckled if he had the energy. "No, this bite wound has spread, and the poison is affecting my body, but I'll heal." He looked into her eyes. "Why do you ask? Am I that pathetic?"

She laughed at him. "That was sarcasm. You know, because you were being nice and said thank you? Non-injured, you would have got the tone."

"Hah," he managed to get out. His mind was too foggy to fully make sense of what she'd said.

"Alright, big guy. You gotta help me move you to the bed." She gave him a glare. "I'm weak, remember, and you weigh like . . . three hundred pounds."

He reached deep inside himself, pushing for his divine powers, and used the last of his remaining strength to rise to his feet. He could do this. He leaned into Mya and stepped out of the shower. She struggled and pulled, just about dragging him across the floor as she finally got him into bed.

CHAPTER SEVENTEEN

MYA

It felt as if Lir weighed a thousand pounds. After the rigorous day of training, Mya found it difficult to help the massive god into bed. She found a pair of his boxers and slid them over his well-toned legs, pointedly trying to ignore his well-endowed penis. That was a feat in itself. His skin was hot to the touch, and that concerned her.

She wasn't sure if he needed medicine or something else. "You're burning up. Do gods get fevers?"

"Yes, but medicine won't help me. My body will burn it out soon enough." He sounded a bit loopy as he spoke.

"Ok. I'll bring you some soup." She wasn't sure if that would work, but some of her foster parents gave her soup when she was sick, and it always made her feel better.

Mya ran to the kitchen and searched through the pantry until she found a lone can of chicken noodle soup in the corner. She dumped it in a bowl and returned to Lir with her heart pounding through her chest.

She plumped up the pillows, leaned him back, and fed him a spoonful.

Lir's face turned into a grimace that looked like he might gag. Had she made it wrong?

"I can't eat," he said with a gentle smile. "Thank you for trying, though."

"Ok. I'll let you sleep. Call me if you need anything."

In the distance, Mya heard the other Guardians arriving. They were probably concerned about Lir. She would hurry and let them know he was healing.

Mya hopped off the bed and took a bite of the soup. Bitter liquid exploded around her taste buds. She forced back a gag. *Okay, it's disgusting.* She could admit that to herself.

He grabbed her wrist as she moved toward the door. "Stay with me," he pleaded.

His request shocked her. She had trouble believing Lir ever asked for much in the way of emotional support.

"Sure, let me just check on the other Guardians, and I'll be back."

He nodded his agreement and lay back down.

In the living room, the other Guardians were cleaning up their weapons and whispering between each other. Mya's gaze roved over their disheveled bodies. They were covered in blood and . . . pieces of flesh? Yes, flesh.

Do not puke! she pleaded with herself.

She tore her gaze away from the bits of body tissue in their hair, clothes, and, well, everywhere. Bile rose into her throat. With great effort, she pushed it back down. She needed a stronger stomach, or she'd be sick all the time around this crew. Finn picked a piece of brain out of his hair and tossed it away. Her stomach did a little flip in protest, but she ignored it.

"What happened?" she asked.

Jari sat at the kitchen table, cleaning her blade. "Vryko-lakas are very, very bad news and extremely hard to kill."

"What the hell are Vrykolakas?" Mya asked.

Alex gave her a brief rundown of the monsters and the events.

"So, these Vrykolakas take a lot of time and effort to kill, Zeus makes them do his bidding, and they attacked in a public shopping mall?"

Jari walked over to the sink and washed the blood off her hands. "Yep."

"The media will be going crazy by now!" Mya said. "The humans don't know about any of this stuff, and Zeus just unleashed his monsters onto them."

"Got that right." Finn snorted and headed over to the sink for his turn to wash the blood off his hands.

The sink turned red, but Mya was too deep in thought to care.

"What are the chances he'll have more monsters at his disposal, ready to throw at the humans?" she asked.

"Likely, but he'll wait a while. He'll want the humans to suffer, so he'll drag this out, unleashing small attacks here and there," Alex said. "Could be years before he attacks again."

"How is Lir?" Jari asked.

Finn dried his hands with a towel. "Aye, he looked a little green around the gills."

"He was bitten by one of those things, and he's pretty weak. I got him into bed, and he says he'll heal."

Jari nodded. "He will. They can't kill us with their bite, just considerably weaken us for a bit."

Alex stood, and bits of flesh fell off his lap, striking the floor with a sickening, wet sound. "I'm headed to the shower and then bed. Don't bother me."

Jari stood as well and stretched one blood-soaked arm. "I'm hungry. The sweet victory of battle has me positively ravenous."

Finn followed her to the granite counter. "I'm hungry, too. I'll make something. You can't cook for shit." He pulled a pan out of the cupboard. He spotted Mya's soup on the counter and helped himself but promptly spit it out. "Bloody hell! Who made this gobshite?"

"Um, I did. It's just a can of soup I found in the pantry." Mya folded her arms across her chest.

"Aye, but love, tell me you at least checked the date on the can?"

She shook her head.

Jari walked to the trash bin and pulled out the can. "Yep, expired. I didn't even know we had cans of soup."

Finn shrugged and dumped out the fetid contents of the bowl. "That's because you never cook. Lir only makes home-made soup. He's a bit of a snob. Can't blame him, though. Canned soup tastes bad, even when it's not expired."

Jari shrugged. "I eat my soup out of the can, and personally, I don't see a problem with it."

Finn flashed a grin. "That's why you aren't allowed to cook, and now we can add Mya to the list as well."

"Jeez, make one bad bowl of soup . . ." Mya scoffed.

Jari nudged Finn in the shoulder. "That's not fair. Mya used to work in a diner, right?"

"Yes, but in Finn's defense, I can't really cook. Just eggs and toast. I can make that."

Finn pulled some items out of the fridge. "No worries. I'll just whip something up real quick like, and we can all be happy."

"Ok, call me when you're done," Mya said. "I'm gonna go check on Lir."

Finn nodded. Jari sauntered over to the table and started wiping down weapons. Mya took that as a dismissal.

She tiptoed out of the kitchen and headed back to Lir's room. She paused at the door and gave it a gentle push. It slid open without making a sound. She blew out a breath and peeked into the room. Lir lay against the pillows with his eyes closed. She eased her body onto the bed and leaned over him.

For a few moments, she watched his face. She'd never noticed the length of his black lashes, the perfect curve to his well-sculpted mouth, or the way one eyebrow seemed to never quite relax. Even in his sleep, he looked worried. She leaned closer, inhaling the scent of the sea and the lingering smell of cloves.

She wondered if he was breathing. His skin looked so pale, and his chest seemed still. Feeling a little panicked, she placed her ear against his chest.

He jerked his eyes open and let out a startled yell.

She reared back and placed her hands up in a calming gesture. "Sorry, sorry. I was just . . . well . . . I wanted to make sure you were breathing."

He leaned back against the pillows and gave her a tiny nod. She scooted up the bed and lay back against the pillow next to him. Her gaze wandered over his strong body, unable to shake the concern that he wouldn't get better.

As her eyes drifted lower, she spotted a pool of blood gathering under his right thigh. "Do you need bandages? Your leg is bleeding quite a bit."

"No, I'll be fine. I heal really fast, and I already feel a little stronger."

"These Vrykolakas are bad news, huh? I mean, obviously they are if you're wounded."

He smiled out of the corner of his mouth. "Yes, they're

hard to kill, and their bites can wound even those who possess divine blood." He cleared his throat. "Jari is a little more immune. Their bites can wound her, but her skin is harder to penetrate, and she's incapable of getting poisoned."

"So, theoretically, Jari is the only one who can defeat them."

Lir scowled. "I can beat them just fine. If those fuckers hadn't bitten me, I would've killed more."

Note to self: Don't fuck with Lir's pride.

"Sorry, I meant she can keep fighting. She won't get wounded too badly or have to stop if she's bitten."

Lir cocked his head to the side. "Yes."

"Have you fought them before?"

"A long time ago. I'm not sure how long. But yes, I had to fight them before. Back then my wi—" He turned red and stopped talking. He blew out a breath and closed his eyes.

Mya waited for a moment before speaking. "It's ok. You don't have to talk about your wife if you don't want to. I didn't even know you had a wife. I guess it makes sense that you'd want to protect her. I mean, by not, uh . . . mentioning her."

Lir's blue eyes popped back open. "I suppose I can't get any fucking rest with all your jabbering. So fine, I'll tell you about my bitch of a wife. Then I want to sleep."

"Okay," she whispered.

Lir rummaged through his nightstand, pulling out his cigarettes and lighting one. "I don't have a wife anymore. It's been a long time since I last saw Aoife. Centuries ago." Lir exhaled a puff of smoke. "We didn't marry for love. Back then, people married for power, and the gods were just the same. But when I married her, I made a promise to myself that I would try my best to love her anyway and to never cheat on her. Loyalty is important to me, and I thought my wife deserved that from me more than anyone. And in time, I did . . . love her." His eyes turned hard and cold as he drew in another puff of his cigarette. "Turns out she never grew to love me, though, and she cheated on me our entire marriage. I suppose it's my fault." He laughed hollowly. "For being a cold bastard."

Mya sat up in bed and turned her body so she could stare into his oceanic eyes. They swirled with power, reminding her of a storm on the horizon.

"Don't say that. You may be a cold bastard, but that doesn't mean you don't deserve a woman to love every cold, rude part of you. Because you aren't just cold. You protect people. You wouldn't be that way if you lacked a heart."

He stubbed out his cigarette and looked at her with softening eyes and a kind smile. Her heart melted. As did her vagina.

He leaned in closer, bringing with him the scent of the sea and cigarettes. Her stomach turned, nausea welled up, and she bolted out of bed. She raced to the toilet, leaned over, and heaved.

Lir ambled into the bathroom, looking pale and sweaty. The blood on his thigh had dried. "Fucking hell, woman. Why do you vomit so much?"

"Soup," she mumbled, and placed her head on the cool tile floor.

"What?"

Mya moaned. "The soup. It was expired."

"Ah, now I know why it was so disgusting." Lir chuckled and scooped her up in his arms. He let out a low groan that made her feel a little guilty.

She was supposed to be taking care of him this time.

Lir dropped her on the bed, and she bounced on the mattress.

"Ow! Why the hell couldn't you set me down gently? I take it back!"

Lir smirked and sank into the bed with another groan. "Take what back?"

"Everything. Taking care of you, saying those nice things about—" Mya gagged and leaned over the bed. Vomit spewed out, drenching the pristine tile floors with a pool of yellowish liquid.

Lir held back her hair and whispered into her ear. "Thank you for making me expired soup that I won't throw up because I'm not a weak little bitch."

Mya halfheartedly slapped at his head, but her hand missed. He yanked her by the hair and dropped her back onto the bed. She covered her head, ready for him to do what, she wasn't sure, because he surprised her with a full-bodied laugh.

She lowered her arms, peeking out to look at him. "Why are you laughing? I just threw up my guts on your floor and tried to hit you in the head. You should be mad!"

"I'm laughing at your adorable attempt to hit me. We need to train you more."

Mya started shivering, her stomach burning. "Why did I get food poisoning? I thought I was a goddess. Or so you keep saying."

Lir pulled the blanket over her body and tucked her in. He was shaking slightly, probably because he was the wounded one. "I suspect all your powers were bound, or whatever the witch said. You still have some healing powers, though, or the bite on your breast wouldn't have healed so well."

Mya smiled. "Were you checking out my boobs, Lir?"

He turned red. "Of course not. I mean, I had to make sure you healed."

"Right."

Lir scowled. "I can't stand your teeth chattering." He slipped under the covers and scooted in closer, wrapping her chilled body with his hot one.

She smiled to herself, tucking her chin below the covers so he wouldn't notice. She felt safer than she had in weeks. Within moments, she dozed off, safe in the arms of a god.

CHAPTER EIGHTEEN

JARI

Covered in blood, Jari headed to her preferred shower in Lir's bathroom. She wouldn't degrade herself by showering in the same stall as those ingrates, Finn and Alex. They were both pigs, not to mention how often they probably jacked off in there. On the other hand, Lir kept his shower clean, and she was fairly certain he feared using his hand for pleasure. Instead, he would just go months without a release and punish everyone with his foul mood and cigarettes.

She faltered as she spotted Lir and Mya in the bed together. They looked so sweet. She felt a little like an intruder, but she had to wash the blood off and couldn't really sleep in her bed like this. She tiptoed to the bathroom and faltered again. Blood covered Lir's normally spotless lavatory like something right out of a horror flick. She supposed there was no reason to interrupt their sleep and shower in here now. Resigned, she collected her shampoo and headed upstairs to the semen-infested bathroom.

She stood in the hot waterfall and let it soothe her. The

Vrykolakas were bad news. Very bad news. They were just about impossible to kill, faster than some gods, and deadlier, too. What would happen if Zeus unleashed the thousands or more monsters at his disposal? Chaos, that's what. Death, death, and more death. It would mean the demise of every Guardian as well as the new girl, Mya.

She shoved down the grief that pressed into her at the thought of losing them. She needed to be strong. They were humanity's only hope, but Jari wasn't so sure they could handle an entire army of Vrykolakas.

Despite the heat of the water, she shivered as she thought about how close she'd come to lying wounded in bed. Those things attempted to tear into her the second they could, but being a goddess of snakes meant her skin was plated with scales just below the surface of her soft flesh, making it much harder to penetrate.

She shrugged off her depressing thoughts as she dried her body and started to brush her hair. She stopped when she caught her reflection in the mirror. Her hair was green! She let out a shriek. Her hair was her pride and joy, and now it was *green!*

What in the actual fuck?

She searched around the bathroom, looking for a culprit. Her shampoo? Someone pulled a prank on her and put dye in the bottle, and that someone was gonna *die!*

Naked as a blue jay, she flung open the bathroom door, slamming it against the wall. "Which one of you cock suckers put dye in my shampoo?" she yelled.

Finn stepped out of his room, eyes wide. He took in her appearance and doubled over in laughter.

"Not funny," she seethed.

"Sorry, love. Shocked me, is all." He was still grinning and laughing slightly. "You still look beautiful."

"Sucking up to me is not going to save you," Jari said.

Mya came barreling up the stairs and froze at the sight of her.

"Oh no, the Head and Shoulders—" Mya started.

Jari turned a burning gaze to her new best friend. *"You did this?"*

Mya stuttered. "Um . . . here's the thing! I, uh . . . thought it was Lir's shamp—"

Jari banshee shrieked and threw herself at Mya. Overcome with rage, she wrapped her hands around her neck. She couldn't control her anger. Distantly, she knew she was hurting her friend, but she couldn't seem to reach that part of herself.

⚜

MYA

MYA SPUTTERED AND stared in shock as her friend choked her. She scrambled, her hands clawing into Jari's, trying to pry them off somehow.

Jari wouldn't kill me just because of her hair, right? she thought frantically.

She stared in horror as Jari's body transformed. Her legs twisted together until they melded into one boneless leg. The lone leg twisted and grew until it became the lower half of a snake. The tail crashed into the floor with a resounding boom. Her torso remained human. Luminescent green scales covered her skin. Her nostrils became slits, her eyes shifted into something reptilian, and sharp fangs protruded from her mouth.

Mya's heart raced in her chest. If she lived through this, she would never touch that woman's hair again.

"Help," she choked out.

Finn was hunched over laughing.

The bastard thinks my dying is funny, does he? She would remember that . . . if she lived long enough. She could feel the air leaving her body, her throat tightening as she became light-headed.

A door at the end of the hall crashed to the ground. Alex stood there, at least a foot taller than his normal mountainous height. Steam billowed out of his nostrils, and his skin was tinged red. Leathery crimson wings sprouted out of his back, and his hands and feet turned into long black talons.

"Let her go, Jari," he commanded in a voice Mya didn't quite recognize.

Jari hissed, squeezing tighter and choking the remaining life from her. She vaguely saw what she thought were flames coming from Alex's mouth before her consciousness departed, bleak darkness winning out.

☙❧

ALEX

ALEX WAS SHOCKED. Jari had transformed into her god-form, and he couldn't understand why the hell she was attacking Mya like a lunatic. He had to act. Mya was passing out. He let his body partially transform into the dragon and lunged toward them. He opened his jaws, clutching Jari with his sharp teeth. They wouldn't harm her, anyway. Mya fell to the ground in a heap. Jari slithered out of his jaws, wrapped her tail around him, and smashed him into the wall.

"Jari," he bellowed, "stop it, you crazy bitch. What's wrong with you?"

She hissed in response and bit into him. A sharp pain tore

into his shoulder, and blood rained down on him. The poison wiggled into his bloodstream. His shoulder was gonna ache like a son of a bitch and damned if he would ask that witch to heal him.

That's it. He wasn't playing around anymore. He conjured a dagger that could pierce Jari's tough, snake-like skin. It was made from a god's bones, dipped in the blood of a gorgon, and had been fashioned into a karambit. He kept it in his arsenal for special occasions when Jari was on her period—or whatever got her pissed off. He never really knew.

Women were fickle.

The dagger would harm her, but only for a little while. She would bitch and moan the whole time she healed, of course, but it would be worth it.

He slashed across her arm and waited for her to notice, hoping the location was one she wouldn't complain about as much. It only took a moment before she screeched, temporarily affecting his eardrums and drenching him in saliva.

"Aw, come on! I just showered!"

Jari backed off, transforming into a woman once again. A naked one, he noticed with appreciation. *Damn, if I knew she was naked, I would've prolonged the battle a bit.*

"Why'd you stab me, Alex?" she wailed.

"Are you freaking kidding me? You attacked Mya!"

A brief look of confusion crossed her face before a horrified expression took its place, seeming to snap her out of her anger. "Oh god! Mya? What have I done?" Jari ran to her and lifted her with a gentle hand, checking her vitals. "She's ok, I think."

Out of nowhere, a swirl of ocean water flooded the floor. Lir was here.

Great. Like we needed two people on their rag to be here right now.

"Everything's fine, boss. Jari got a little upset over her hair and attacked Mya, but Alex took care of it," Finn said, trying to de-escalate the situation. "Mya's fine."

Lir wasn't calmed down by Finn's statement. He leveled Jari with a vicious glare. "You attacked Mya? Over your *hair?*"

Jari at least had the decency to look sheepish. "I was really tired and couldn't control my god-form." She splayed her hands. "She came out as soon as I got upset. I tried to push her back, but I couldn't contain it."

Lir relaxed a bit. He would have understood that logic. They all had trouble containing their god-forms sometimes. He gently shook Mya awake.

She sat up, slightly coughing. "What happened?" she asked, her voice hoarse.

Jari threw her arms around her neck, crying. "I'm so sorry, Mya. I didn't mean to. I just lost control, and my god-form is a bit crazy when she's angry. I didn't mean to hurt you. Please forgive me!"

Mya patted Jari's head in reassurance. "It's okay if you didn't mean to. I forgive you. Plus, I did accidentally dye your hair green. It was meant for Lir." She pointed over to their fearless leader. "I was mad at him, and I thought the Head & Shoulders shampoo was his."

"Well, it is a man's shampoo," Finn added.

Jari crossed her arms defensively. "I like the smell, okay?"

Lir stared at Mya, a look of contempt on his face. "You were mad at me and decided to put dye in my shampoo? You thought that was a good form of vengeance?"

"Yes? Like I said, I was mad at you. What's wrong with

my idea? I thought it was brilliant." Mya finished her statement with her arms crossed.

"Totally brilliant," Jari added, clearly trying to get back on her good side.

Lir snorted. "I don't give a flying fuck what color my hair is. Next time you're pissed at me, sweetheart, just stab me."

"Really? I have permission to stab you?" Mya asked with a hopeful look in her eyes.

"Sure, why not? It won't hurt me, and it's much better than your other hair-brained idea."

Alex rolled his eyes.

"Fine, sleep with one eye open, Lir," she taunted.

He brushed off her comment. At least she seemed to be recovering.

Lir pointed around the catastrophe zone. "One of you idiots go ask Hecate to clean up this mess. You were all so happy to tear up the walls and doors in your little tryst." With that statement, he walked away, trails of water swirling after him.

They all grumbled and groaned.

CHAPTER NINETEEN

MYA

Mya headed to Hecate's room and gave a gentle knock. Hecate opened the door with a mask covering her eyes.

"Um, hi. We need some magical clean up."

Hecate lifted the eye mask and surveyed the room with her peculiar purple eyes. Mya took a moment to observe Hecate's eccentric pajamas. She wore an odd assortment of clothing: a nightgown coupled with bright-pink flannel pants. Bunny slippers adorned her feet, and her hair was in old-fashioned curlers. And she thought Jari was weird.

"You woke me up for this?" Hecate scoffed. "I could fix this in my sleep."

She waved her hand, and Mya felt the surge of magic wash over her, leaving her skin all tingly. The magic felt pleasant this time, not dark. She shuddered, remembering the last time Hecate used magic on her. She watched in fascination as walls repaired themselves, the carpet dried, and the door righted itself back into the frame.

A grin lit up Alex's face. "That little trick makes hanging out with the witches worth it." He winked at Hecate. "Almost."

Hecate muttered something in reply but was too tired to do much else. She headed back to her room to sleep.

Mya turned to Jari. "So you all have these god-forms that you turn into?"

Jari nodded.

"You turn into a snake, and Alex is a dragon," Mya said with confidence. She was pretty sure she'd figured that much out.

"Yes," Jari said.

"What about Lir and Finn?"

"Finn turns into a giant tree with tree trunk legs and arms. Lir turns into a sea monster with tentacles for legs. You don't want to see his form." Jari shuddered. "It's pretty gross."

Mya would take her word for it. It sounded gross. "Are you all more powerful afterward?"

"Yes, we are."

"Why don't you use that form more often? Did Lir use his form when you fought earlier?"

"No, we try not to use it because once we transform back into our human bodies, we're fatigued and vulnerable. If we were in another realm, it wouldn't be a problem, but on Earth, it's a weakness," Jari explained.

"There are other realms?"

"Yes. There's the god realm, the realm of angels, a realm for demons, and a spirit realm. I imagine there are more, but that's all I know about," said Jari.

There was so much Mya didn't know. She wondered if she could visit all the different realms. She thought of the underworld that she saw in her vision from Nyx. Could it be one of the realms Jari mentioned?

"What is the underworld part of?" she asked.

Jari looked a little surprised at her question. "The underworld is the demon realm. Some gods do stay there, though. It's mostly known as the underworld instead of the demon realm because it belonged to the gods first."

Interesting.

Jari squeezed Mya's shoulder. "I'm sorry, but I really need to rest now. Talk later?" She looked so vulnerable, and Mya understood now why they didn't transform so often.

"Yeah, talk later. Get some rest." Mya gave her a soft smile, hoping to convey she wasn't upset with her. She wasn't sure why she wasn't more bothered by the scuffle, but deep down, she knew Jari didn't mean to harm her. The gods weren't human, so she couldn't expect them to act like humans.

Jari hugged her again. She was a touchy, feely friend. "Night."

Mya smiled again. "Night."

۞

BIRDS SANG their merry little tunes to each other. Cicadas chirped in the treetops and insects buzzed about. Mya wiped sweat off her neck for the thousandth time that day as the sun blazed hotter than what she assumed hell might feel like. Unfortunately, she was stuck out here in the damn forest. If she never saw another forest again, she wouldn't complain.

"Hit me harder!" Alex growled.

"I am hitting hard!" She threw another punch into the focus mitt.

Alex didn't move a single muscle as he looked at her with an unimpressed expression and one eyebrow raised.

"First of all, no, you are not. You need to use your whole

body when you throw your punch. Second of all, I told you to close your fist and place your thumb over the knuckles, not under them."

"Right." Mya grumbled, dropped her fist, and took a large gulp of air. *Okay, you can do this. Use your whole body and close your fist properly,* she pep-talked herself.

"We don't have all day." He held the focus mitt in front of her face as if she'd forgotten what she was supposed to be doing.

"I know. I just need a moment. Jeez."

"Fine." Alex dropped the mitt, stepping closer to her.

"Do you mind if I touch you? I want to help you learn how to use your body."

She appreciated that he'd asked—though, most of the time, the gods were all pretty touchy feely. She nodded at him. He nodded back and stepped behind her. He planted her feet on the ground and adjusted her elbows.

"Okay. Throw your punch," he ordered as he stepped back to watch her.

She checked her fist for proper form and threw her arm out in a forward motion.

Alex stepped back into her personal space and grabbed her hips. "Throw it again, but this time, slightly twist your hips and rotate your back leg. This enables you to use all your strength."

She threw another punch into the air as Alex directed her body.

"Better. Next time, don't throw your arm out too far. Keep it fairly close to your body."

He stepped back in front of her with the focus mitt. Each time she threw a punch, he'd yell, "Again!" In no time, her arms were aching and burning, and even more sweat covered her.

Alex called a time-out and threw the mitts into his duffle bag. As he turned to speak, Jari appeared, the portal spitting her out. She didn't falter and continued walking toward them with a powerful strut.

She waved at them and said, "We gotta go. I found a potential ally, and Lir wants everyone there."

Alex nodded and picked up the training gear. Mya followed suit, and they headed back to the safe house.

"Took you long enough," Lir growled from the living room sofa. He'd changed from his normal suit to black leather pants and a leather jacket, his favorite sword strapped to his back.

Mya liked the change.

Jari rolled her eyes at him. "I was only gone five minutes at the most."

Lir ignored her. "I found a potential ally. She works within the military. After a lot of searching, I finally uncovered her at a naval base."

"Is she a goddess?" Alex asked as he emptied the duffel bag and started checking the weapons.

Lir sighed. "It's Athena."

Alex raked a hand through his hair and looked up at the ceiling. "She'll never agree to help us. She hates me."

"I know, but we have to try."

"Why does Athena hate you? And isn't she Zeus's daughter? Why would she help us?" Mya asked with a small voice.

Alex ejected a clip from the handgun he held and began filling it with bullets. "Athena is my sister. Our parents pitted us against each other our entire childhood. We continued that feud for many centuries after we left our parents, causing mass destruction to just about everything and everyone we were associated with. We finally reached an uneasy alliance and decided to avoid each other entirely. She won't welcome my presence." He looked at Lir as he said this last.

Lir nodded. "That's why I want everyone to go."

"You don't need me. It's risky," Alex countered.

"I can handle a couple of war gods," Hecate said as she strolled into the room wearing a long purple robe covered in zebra stripes.

Alex raised a brow. "Wearing that?"

"My outfit doesn't affect my powers, moron." Hecate scoffed.

Alex laughed, surprising Mya. He rarely said anything nice around Hecate, and he certainly didn't laugh around her.

"Fair point. Thank you for agreeing to this," he said with a nod, surprising Mya yet again.

She looked around and everyone else was also staring at Alex with their mouths open wide in shock.

"Let's do this," Jari said, breaking the silence.

They all nodded and finished getting ready.

❧

Filled with boredom, Mya walked around the office. Passing an oak desk, she spotted a terrarium in the corner with a spider in it. *Eck, who the hell keeps a spider as a pet?* Even more odd were the crocheted doilies scattered around and placed in the most random spots. She even found one affixed to the window. Shaking her head at the mustard brown doily on the bookshelf, she paused and studied the framed certificates adorning the walls in the tidy little office.

They were here to see Athena, the goddess of military strategy. Athena was now calling herself Colonel Kendra Adamson. Mya wasn't sure what to think of her or what would happen, but one thing was clear: she was a tremendously successful and decorated veteran.

She stepped away from the certificates and sank between Jari and Hecate on the worn leather couch against one of the office walls. Alex, Finn, and Lir leaned against the walls in different corners, filling the room with massive waves of testosterone. The office was starting to feel claustrophobic.

The door to the office finally clicked open, and they released a collective sigh. Everyone felt as restless as her, if not more. She suspected more since they were all impatient gods who were used to quickly getting their way.

A woman who looked like a prettier version of Alex stepped into the room. She had the same fierce and fiery eyes, a set of high cheekbones, and sizable biceps that weren't common for most women. A bun secured her long, dark hair to the nape of her neck, and her fatigues looked perfectly unwrinkled. It made sense; everything about this woman screamed stern and fierce.

Lir stepped forward and shook her hand. "Thank you for agreeing to meet us."

She scowled at him. "I agreed to meet *you,* not *him.*" She tilted her head toward Alex, refusing to turn around and look at him.

Lir sighed. "I know, but I need both of you to put aside your differences for this war. Zeus is unleashing chaos, and you two can agree on one thing here."

Kendra cocked a hip. "And what are you assuming we agree on?"

"Your hatred for Zeus. He's our common enemy."

"Our father is an idiot who changes whims every two seconds," Kendra said. "He's been claiming he'll eradicate the humans for hundreds of years, and yet he hasn't. That man never knows what he wants. Besides, he'd be a fool to attack the humans now. They're too advanced. If he starts a war with them, they might set missiles loose. Missiles that would destroy the entire world."

"A few months ago, I would have agreed with you," Lir said, "but he's making moves now. He attacked a ship off the coast of Italy. I'm sure you know this already."

She nodded.

"He also set loose the Vrykolakas on a bunch of humans at a mall," Lir continued.

She sucked in a breath. "The Vrykolakas?" She looked around at the rest of the room and frowned. "Is this it? *This* is your army that will stop the king of the gods and an army of Vrykolakas?"

Lir nodded grimly. "Yes, this is it."

"You need more than this. Who else have you contacted?"

"So far, it's us"—he gestured around the room—"and hopefully you. That's all we've got."

Kendra groaned and started pacing as she mumbled to herself. Finally, she stopped and addressed Lir. "I'll gather a small group of the best soldiers. Keep in mind, they're human and will need protection. With the right weapons, I can set them up as snipers a safe distance from the battle. It has to be a small group, though. We can't have the humans knowing about this. Don't call me for your little battles, either. You call me when Zeus is present, and that's it. Got it?"

"Yes." Lir shook her hand.

She turned to leave the room and stopped in front of Alex. "I hate you."

"I know, but I think we can put aside our differences to deal with him."

"If dealing with you means we stop a full-on war of the gods, then I'll do it."

"Good."

"Fine." She huffed.

Alex looked at her with a devilish smirk. "I love you."

Kendra reared her arm back and slammed him in the gut.

He glared at her as he hunched over and clutched his abdomen protectively. "What . . . the . . . hell?"

Kendra smiled. "Do I need a reason, brother?" She patted his cheek rather hard. "And I love you too."

Lir looked at Hecate, who nodded and waved her hand, transporting them all back to the safe house . . . just like magic.

CHAPTER TWENTY

MYA

Mya pushed the food around her plate. She should've been more than happy to devour homemade lasagna. Not even the mouth-watering aroma could compel her to eat. Her training sessions with Alex had been brutal. Come to think of it, brutal was too kind a word, but she was too tired to think of something more fitting.

Alex had pushed her past her limit, day in and day out. She came home covered in dirt, branches, and all kinds of things. Too sore to move a muscle, she often found herself asleep on the floor where the portal had pushed her out. She couldn't deny the effectiveness of the training, though. She was getting stronger, her endurance lasted longer, and she could see the beginnings of some muscle tone.

A loud banging on the front door startled her from her thoughts.

"Who in the name of Zeus is pounding on the door?" Jari wrenched it open, katana in hand, fierce battle face on. "Hermes?" she asked, bewildered.

"Harold now," he corrected.

Jari smirked and cocked her hip. "Great name. Should I call you Harry? You look like a Harry."

"Sure." His facial expression didn't change as he shrugged his shoulders. He gestured inside. "Care to let me in? I've got lots of errands to run. I'm still a messenger, you know."

"Yeah, fine. Come on in." She waved him in and stepped aside.

Harold didn't look like Mya expected. There was no golden helmet, winged booties, or a scepter in hand. He looked like a teenage boy with blond, longish curls, a skinny build, and bright-blue eyes. He wore a Metallica t-shirt and jeans with a ripped-for-fashion look. He wasn't perfect or beautiful like the Guardians. The old eyes that seemed to hold eons of intelligence in just one glance were the only things that made her think "god." Perhaps being the messenger allowed him to hold all that knowledge—the secrets he must possess and keep hidden. It gave her shivers just thinking about it. She wouldn't want that task.

Lir came into the kitchen through the back door, hair still wet with seawater. The salty, crisp scent flowed toward her. Finn was close in his wake, holding a handful of tomatoes like one would hold a lover.

"Ah, Finn, were you rescuing your tomatoes again?" Jari teased.

Finn clutched his tomatoes possessively. "Damn birds keep eating all my fresh grown vegetables. Do you know how much love and care I give to my garden? Hmm? You don't. If you did, you would be out there saving them with me!" He huffed and started washing them tenderly while cooing to them.

It was a very odd scene, and Mya wasn't sure why he cared so much. Surely the god of plants could just grow more?

Lir scrubbed his hand over his face, annoyed with them already. "We have an audience, children. Save the bickering for later."

He turned to address their guest. "Hermes, welcome to our home."

"It's Harold now, actually. I'm no longer Hermes and don't answer to that name."

"Right, my apologies." Lir gave him a tight smile.

"None taken, my lord. It's an honor to bring you messages." He bowed to Lir.

Mya was a little shell-shocked. Harold was a god, too. Why was he bowing?

Lir was unfazed by the act of respect. "And whose message are you passing?"

Harold hastened to stand up and pulled a glittering golden letter out of nowhere. He handed it to Lir. "Regrettably. I come with news from Zeus, and I'm afraid he's lost his marbles a wee bit."

Lir folded his arms across his chest. "I would tell you just how I feel about that, Harold, but frankly, I don't trust you not to turn around and tell Zeus what I said."

"Now, why would I do such a thing?" Harold feigned insult and clutched his chest. "The Guardians are protectors and not to be played with as the other gods are."

"Save it for someone who believes you. We all know you love to start wars with your gossiping and your messages," Lir said, brow raised.

"Very true words, Harry." Jari snorted.

"Fine, you've caught me!" Harold said. "Can't blame me

for having a little fun. It's so hard, being a messenger for a bunch of gods who all treat you like a slave." He feigned sadness and pouted his lips. "Who could blame me, really?"

Mya could see his logic in that one, but he had to know how much power words could have. Especially in times of war.

"Uh-huh. Can you take a refreshment or food or something and leave us to read your message in peace?" Finn added, apparently done making love to his tomatoes.

Harold crossed his arms. "Fine, I know when I'm not wanted. I suppose I won't be telling you about your potential allies, then. It's no secret Zeus is planning a mass attack on the humans." A knowing smile bloomed across his face.

Don't fall for the bait, guys, Mya thought. There was a moment of tense silence as they all looked at each other.

"What do you want for this knowledge?" Lir asked, breaking the quiet.

Harold blinked once, tilted his head to the side, and said, "Immunity."

"Immunity from what?" Lir asked.

"When Zeus goes crazy and starts killing everyone—well, everyone else—and the four of you decide to protect the mortals, thus starting a war, I want immunity from your vengeance." He looked around the room. "I'm simply a messenger and do not wish to die when, or if, you kill him and whoever else he has at his disposal."

"Will you stop delivering messages to him if we do this for you?" Lir asked.

Harold huffed, crossing his arms again. He looked very much like an angsty teen. "You know I can't go up against Zeus! That would be suicide! I just said I don't want to die, didn't I?"

"Alright, fine. I see your point." Lir looked at Finn and Jari.

Proving themselves mind readers, they both nodded at him.

"We'll grant you immunity as payment for your knowledge on our potential allies." He sighed as he said it, proving he didn't really want to give Hermes—er, Harold—immunity.

"Thank you. You are most gracious, my lord." Harold bowed again, like a perfect little ass kisser.

Lir waved his arms in exasperation. "Go on!"

"Right! Well, the werewolves are still very much against Zeus and would be willing to do just about anything to break their after-death curse." Harold said it like a schoolgirl with juicy gossip. He was referring to the Vrykolakas the Guardians recently fought. If they cured them of their curse, that might tip the war in favor of the Guardians.

"That curse is older than some of us, and the story of the curse is even older," Jari said. "I'm not sure we even possess the power to break a curse of that caliber."

"Yes, but some of the gods were there. They heard the story as it happened, and some of the gods know how to break some of the older curses. Possibly, even the one hiding upstairs?" Harold trailed off at the end in a knowing way.

"Who are you suggesting is hiding upstairs?" Lir asked with a warning growl to his voice.

"Hecate," Harold said, stepping back a bit.

Lir narrowed his eyes at him. "I won't confirm that."

The messenger chuckled. "Be that as it may, she could help the werewolves if you can convince her to, thus gaining you more allies."

Lir scoffed. "I hate to agree with you, but I do. Now, would you happen to be one of these gods with the knowledge to aid Hecate in breaking the werewolves curse?"

Harold cocked a smug half-grin. "I wouldn't release such knowledge. At least, not yet."

"Gods, you are infuriating." Lir pulled out a cigarette and lit it. He took a moment to inhale and relax. "Do you have any more potential allies? Anyone who seems to be against what Zeus is doing?"

"Most of the gods hate humans about as much as Zeus does. When the humans gave up on us, we lost most of our powers. Gods are petty and vengeful," Harold said. After a purposeful pause, he continued. "I know of one. Prometheus. He goes by Aiden now. He was and still is a lover of humans. He would want to aid you."

"Do you know where he is?" Lir asked.

"Perhaps." Harold had grown cocky.

Lir grabbed him in one hand, clutching him by his shirt. *"Tell me where he is!"*

Harold threw his arms up as he lost some of his bravado. "I can't tell you that. To reveal the location of someone I deliver messages to is against the rules," he sputtered. "I cannot go about telling the gods where to find one another. You must find him on your own."

Lir dropped him with a hiss, and he tumbled to the ground. The rest of the Guardians groaned but couldn't argue with his logic. Jari waved her arm in a go-on gesture intended for Harold.

He stood, brushing off his clothes. "Last potential ally that I know of would be the angels. They claim to love the humans and would most likely choose your side."

"The angels are too unpredictable to trust as allies," Jari said. "You never know when they might turn on you."

"Very true," Harold added, looking pensive. "I think in this case, they'll not turn on you. If the humans die, they have no one to worship and pray to them. Sadly, the humans still believe in the angels to some extent. I don't believe they'd want to lose that power."

"Unless the angels have turned their backs on the humans as well," Mya said. "Could their god do that? Would he re-make mortals who do believe in him?"

"That's a myth of the religions the humans currently believe in," Harold continued. "Their 'god' didn't make humans. He made the angels and demons. Zeus created the humans. That's why he's so angry. The humans not only stopped worshipping him, they also no longer give him credit for their existence."

Mya thought back to her Sunday school lessons and cringed. "Is Hell even real?" she asked.

"No, not really," Lir said. "There's the underworld, and Hades is in charge of it, but it's not an eternal place for the damned. It's more of a place for spirits to rest in between phases of life, and some gods reside there too. There's a special section for those souls deemed too evil to be given a host. They stay there in exile and punishment."

"So if someone cheats on their spouse, or steals, or goes against some of the ten commandments, they don't go to Hell once they die?" Mya asked.

Jari grabbed her hand. "No, Mya. The Bible and the commandments aren't real. Only souls who do explicitly horrible things are punished."

"Good to know," Mya continued. "And what about God? Is he or she real?"

Harold answered her this time. "Yes, they have a real name, though I don't know it. The humans worshipping him have given him quite a lot of power, and he's hidden his true identity. Those of us who knew him no longer remember who he is, or like you said, if God is a man or woman. We simply call them the human god."

"We're getting off-topic. Let's focus on the message and lining up some allies," Lir said.

When Mya turned back, she looked around for Harold. "Did the messenger guy leave?"

"Yep. You missed it." Jari smiled. "It's all smoke and mirrors. He knocks on the door to show hospitality, but he doesn't need permission to enter. He can just appear."

How convenient for him, Mya thought.

Harold popped back in, right in front of her. She stepped back and held in her startled scream.

"I thought you left," she said.

"No, I went upstairs." He turned toward Alex and wagged his finger. "Guess what I saw!" he sang.

"What?" Alex said with zero interest.

"I saw a certain witchy goddess in your bedroom, and I'm not quite sure, but it looked like she was spraying your pillow with a potion of some kind."

"She did *what?*" Alex bellowed, and stomped up the stairs.

Jari turned to Harold with a grin and sprayed him with the water bottle she held. "You little troublemaker!"

Harold wiped the water off his face. "But it's so much fun. Did you see his face?" He hunched over from laughter and then pounded his fists against his chest as he imitated Alex. "Me angry!"

Mya laughed. "How did you know Alex doesn't like witches?" Upstairs, she heard loud crashing and banging sounds and assumed Alex and Hecate were fighting.

Harold leaned closer to her. "That's easy. I was there when a witch—"

"Harold!" Alex yelled from upstairs.

"That's my cue. Gotta go." He saluted Mya and disappeared into thin air.

Perfect timing, too. Alex was now downstairs, looking quite furious if the smoke coming out of him was any indication.

CHAPTER TWENTY-ONE

MYA

Lir opened the golden note and started reading aloud:

Dearest Guardians,

It has recently come to my attention that you have interceded on two of my attacks on the mortals. For the sake of all the excellent service you have provided in the past, I must warn you to cease all efforts.

If you heed my warning and leave the mortals to their demise, I will not punish you. However, if you continue to interrupt my attacks (that I planned with excellence), there will be repercussions.

Know this: no one will save you from me, for my wrath is strongest of all the gods, as is my strength. Your aid to the humans will be your undoing, for you will die by my hand.

I wish you all a good day and good luck! Be merry.

With love,

Zeus

Jari snatched the letter. Her hazel eyes moved at a rapid pace as she read it. "Wow, that's so sweet of him."

"Very passive-aggressive," Mya added.

Finn leaned over Jari and tapped the paper aggressively. "We're not listening to this load of bollocks! Who the hell ends a threatening letter with 'be merry' and 'with love'?"

"He doesn't consider it a threat because he feels confident we'll heed his warning," Lir said.

Jari pursed her lips. "Someone should fetch Hecate. We could use her opinion on this."

Hecate's musical voice called from the hallway. "No need. I am already here. I heard the messenger god and the contents of the letter from Zeus." She drifted into the room, her spirit forms trailing after her.

Mya ignored them whenever she could, and she wasn't the only one. The other Guardians ignored them as well. *None more than Alex,* she chuckled to herself.

Which was why he left as quickly as possible. It was hard to watch as they did things Hecate wasn't doing and touched people with their creepy ghost hands. The thought sent a shiver through her body.

Please, God, don't let one of those things touch me. She should probably stop praying to God, now that she thought about it.

Lir addressed Hecate and didn't avoid the spirits as he did so, proving himself the bravest in the bunch. "What do you think of these allies?"

"I think we should seek Aiden first. He will be the easiest to trust and find. He will not have any qualms against fighting Zeus." She smiled at that part. "Aiden also possesses the power of fire, and while it is not that effective against Zeus, it could be useful, among other things."

"Would his fire affect the Vrykolakas?" Jari asked.

Hecate nodded. "Yes, I believe so. He would be very useful for your cause."

Lir drew his brows together. "Okay, so we find him first, but where?"

Hecate waved off his comment. "I should be able to cast a locator spell." She paused. "Though, he is a titan, and if he does not want to be found, even I may not be able to find him."

"I have a feeling he'll want to be found." Lir smirked.

"Yes, the attack of the Vrykolakas should be all over the news by now. He will know what Zeus has done," Hecate said.

"What of the angels? Do we trust them or not?" Lir asked.

The witch furrowed her brow as she pondered his question for a moment. "I think it is best to leave the angels alone for now."

Lir nodded. "Agreed."

"That leaves the curse. How do we break an ancient curse?" Jari asked.

"That will be the hardest task of all, but perhaps the most important at this time." Hecate floated back and forth across the room; it was her version of pacing. "If we can eliminate the Vrykolakas, that will force Zeus to find other monsters and possibly show up himself."

"What do you know about the curse?" Lir asked her.

Hecate looked contemplative. "It has been too long since the curse took place. I must think on it and sift through my memories." She looked at Lir. "Let's find Aiden, and by the time your journey is done, my memory should be restored." Hecate turned to one of her spirits. "Find Alex. I will need him for this spell."

The spirit floated away. Alex wouldn't like being fetched by a spirit, and she suspected he would like to be included in a spell even less. Mya looked forward to the inevitable explosion in three . . . two . . . one . . .

Nothing happened. She waited, fidgeting impatiently. *Come on, Alex.*

The front door slammed into the ground with a bang. The wood splintered, and shards flew everywhere, some of them landing as far as the kitchen. Alex came stomping behind the fragments, a wall of fury. Flames danced in his eyes, veins bulged from his neck, and smoke billowed from his nostrils. Hecate should have been quivering in fear, but she wasn't. She stared Alex down with all the courage of a battle commander. Alex came within inches of Hecate and lifted her by the throat, slamming her into the wall behind them. It splintered as he pushed her further into it.

"Do not *ever* send your goddamn spirits to find me!" Venom saturated his voice, and blistering heat radiated within his eyes.

Hecate smirked right before waving her hand and tossing him into the opposite wall like a rag doll. The wall collapsed into the living room, further littering debris throughout the house. Lir was going to be pissed now, too.

"You want to play, big boy? I can do this all day," Hecate taunted with a hungry smile. Her tone was heated and full of innuendo, not showing the least bit of fear.

Alex stood up and roared. The sound echoed off the walls, vibrating Mya's body. He lunged into the air. Lir and Finn caught him mid-leap, each placing a hand on an arm, and wrestled Alex to the ground.

"Enough!" Lir commanded, squeezing Alex's bicep.

Alex roared again, and wings ripped out of his back.

"Alex! Calm down," Lir tried to reason as he clutched Alex and gritted his teeth. "We need you for the spell. That's why Hecate sent a spirit to find you. If I knew you'd throw a tantrum like this, I would've found you myself." Lir crowded the god of war's vision so he could no longer see the aggravating witch. "Now calm the fuck down."

Alex struggled a bit more, roared again, and then rested his face on the ground. He inhaled and exhaled several deep breaths for a few moments before speaking. "Ok. I'm fine. Get off me!" His voice was a bit hoarse.

Probably from all the growling and roaring, Mya thought.

Finn and Lir released Alex, standing as they did.

Alex stood and gave Hecate a vicious glare. "If you kill me with your creepy ass spell, you best believe I will haunt your ass!"

Hecate smiled and shrugged. "If I can kill you with my spell, then you are no god of war."

His chest puffed up, and the glint in his eyes turned frightening. He was going to flip out again.

"Alex," Lir said, placing a hand on his chest.

Alex pushed his hand away. "I said I'm fine! I'm not going to attack her. Just get this shit over with." He turned his gaze to Hecate. "I don't like it, and while we're at it, tell me what we're doing and why."

Lir explained the visit with Hermes, the letter from Zeus, the potential allies, and how they needed Hecate to cast a locator spell to find Aiden.

"I still don't understand why you need me for this. Are you just trying to torture me or what?" He looked at her, waiting for some explanation.

She smiled serenely. "I need you for the spell because you have the spirit of fire in you. It will help me locate other beings who control fire."

Hecate almost sounded genuine, but Mya had her doubts that it was more than just for his "fire."

"I can't argue that since I don't understand magic, dammit," he muttered.

"Come on, quit being such a baby," Hecate taunted.

If Mya didn't know any better, she'd think Hecate enjoyed giving Alex a hard time.

Alex huffed, blowing smoke out of his nostrils. Hecate's pet snake slithered into the kitchen, managing to avoid the debris in a way that a snake shouldn't. Mya had forgotten all about that thing. Why the hell was it in the house? She fought the sudden vision of Hecate's snake eating her. That thing gave her the creeps.

"Hecate, I told you the pet snake stays outside," Lir said.

Mya let out a sigh of relief. *Thank the gods for small miracles.*

"I know, and I will send him back outside. My little guy must have noticed the open front door and decided to visit his mommy. Didn't you?" She stepped closer to pet the snake, but he slithered past her, heading straight to Jari.

Hecate seemed to have forgotten Jari was a goddess of snakes. They must gravitate to her. Without hesitation, Jari picked up the snake and wrapped it around her body, stroking it. It curled up and fell asleep in her lap.

Lir tilted his head as he studied it. "Fine, it can stay for now. Watch him, Jari."

"Yes, boss," Jari said with a smile.

Hecate's spirits reappeared with different tools. Alex paled. Mya almost laughed at him.

The great god of war, afraid of spirits and witchcraft. Ha!

Hecate cleared the debris from the ground with a wave of her hand and drew a symbol on the floor in chalk. It was round and looked like a compass. She drew different symbols around the points of the compass. They didn't look like the cardinal directions to Mya, but she didn't recognize the symbols, so who knew.

"Symbols of the different realms," Jari told her. She must have caught her staring.

Hecate sat Alex down in the middle of the compass. He was visibly shaking now. She pulled out an athame with a golden handle. The blade looked rusted, though she had a feeling the rust was blood.

"Hold out your hand," Hecate calmly told Alex. She was being gentle with him, considering Mya's own experience with Hecate. She hadn't given a warning before cutting into *her* flesh.

Alex obeyed, and Hecate cut his palm with the blade. She stood and began walking in a circle, dripping the blood onto the ground and chanting.

"Phasmatos insindia meven, phasmatos insindia meven." She chanted louder. *"Phasmatos insindia meven!"*

Alex clutched his weapon with a crushing grip, his hands turning white, but he didn't leave his assigned spot in the circle. His bravery outweighed his fear.

One of the symbols on the floor started glowing white, pulsing as if to say, "I am here." Hecate honed her attention on the glowing symbol and continued chanting.

She stopped and looked up.

Her once lavender eyes were completely white, and she spoke in a voice that was hers but not hers. "I have found him." She pulled out a hand-held mirror that appeared as ancient as the athame. She conjured an image of Aiden's location and showed it to the group. "He is here. You must open the portal and hurry. I cannot hold it. He does not want to be found, and the witch who hid him is powerful."

Hecate started to sway as Lir opened the portal. She ended the spell and let out a heavy sigh. The magic dissipated, creating a vacuum effect. Even the air left the room in a *whoosh.* Alex stopped shaking and struggled to stand. He refused Lir's and Jari's help, every inch the warrior.

Lir looked around, deciding who would go and who would stay.

Hecate made his decision for him. "We must all go. The magic told me so."

He looked like he wanted to argue, but didn't. Since Hecate was the only one who understood magic, if she said the magic told her they must all go, then they must.

Lir released a begrudged sigh. "Grab your weapons. Let's go."

Alex pulled out a holster, a gun, and ammo, his hands still shaking a bit. He handed it to Mya with a nod of affirmation. She hastened to put the holster on and checked the gun.

Loaded. Good.

Finn tied his axe to his back while Jari released the large snake to the ground and checked her katanas. They were ready. Hecate swayed dangerously; the spell had weakened her. The witch fell into Finn. He caught and cradled her gently in his arms.

Lir stepped into the portal with Jari just behind him. Finn followed, cradling Hecate in his arms. Mya took a deep breath and stepped through next. She braced herself for the spinning, falling, and blackness that she hated with a passion. Eventually, she'd get it and travel through the portal as the Guardians did. Gracefully.

CHAPTER TWENTY-TWO

MYA

They arrived in front of a seemingly normal suburban home. The two-story colonial-style house was painted an HOA-approved white and had two picture-perfect windows. Rose bushes lined the outside, finishing off the quaint appearance. No one would guess that a god lived here. A typical family with two-and-a-half kids, a cat, and a dog? Yes. But a god? No.

Lir barged ahead of them. His boots made a wet sound as he stomped across the moist grass. He rolled up the sleeves of his royal-blue dress shirt, allowing a view of his ancient tattoos. They swirled around his arms, reminding Mya of the rise and fall of the ocean tide. Done rolling up his sleeves, he whipped out his longsword from where it sat tied against his back and swung it around the air.

Jari laughed from where she stood behind him and pulled a small knife from her thigh-high boots. "Expecting trouble, boss? Should I ready my weapons?" she asked, zipping open her leather jacket to reveal the dual katanas hanging from her belt.

"Not yet."

"Fine." Jari pouted her lips and tightened the elastic around her now green hair. The wind whipped against her swishing ponytail, filling the air with her jasmine perfume.

Finn's combat boots clomped against the earth as he followed behind Jari, the light breeze tousling his shoulder-length blond hair. The scent of his black leather jacket filled Mya's nose. He still held Hecate within his arms, her green velvet dress clashing with the more modern styles of the group. The bell sleeves of her gown billowed around the axe attached to Finn's waist.

Alex stalked through the night like a silent wraith, his eyes missing nothing as he scanned the horizon. He hunched down, running a hand through the grass. The moonlight sparkled against his scalp, highlighting his closely cropped brown hair. Seemingly satisfied with his check, he stood and brushed the dirt from his leather pants, then strolled off to the side. His every step was light, precise, and utterly silent. If Mya didn't trust him, she'd never want that man at her back.

Mya trudged across the ground, wearing jeans, Converse, and a hoodie. She needed some help from Jari on how to dress like a badass Greek goddess. Or maybe she'd find a book on it. She might even use her experience to write one herself. Except, who would buy it? Her mind was drifting into ridiculous thoughts again.

Focus, Mya! You're about to approach a god—uninvited!

LIR

Lir knocked on the door politely. Alex and Jari disappeared into the night in different directions to scan the outside perimeter and check for threats. The whole "element of surprise" strategy.

Lir waited patiently, but no one came to the door. The night was silent. He carefully turned the knob and was met with zero resistance. He eased the door open and waited a moment. Still silent. He moved further in and scanned the room from left to right. Aside from a grand staircase, the foyer stood empty.

They moved into the parlor room. Also empty.

Odd.

He started to walk into the foyer but stopped at the entryway to the kitchen. He stood in the corner and beckoned Finn into the empty room. Mya sidled up next to him, being cautious and quiet. Finn handed Hecate off to Lir and crept into the living room and then the kitchen. He held a gun in front of him with steady hands. Lir hated guns and refused to use them. Though he knew they could be useful, he preferred his traditional weapons.

"Clear," Finn whispered back to them.

He returned, and they started up the stairs in a single file line with Lir in front and Finn in back, protecting Mya and Hecate. The hall bathroom was empty. Lir could see that much. Why was the entire house so desolate? No furniture? Nothing.

Is Aiden using magic to hide himself? And how did he know we were coming?

He *was* the god of forethought. Maybe he foresaw their visit and hid, but why? Did he not want to help? Did he no longer care for the humans?

Lir made his way down the hallway with cautious steps. He stopped next to a door. Using the same method as before, he stood in the corner and watched Finn's back as he entered the room. His gun was drawn and ready. This room was empty as well. They repeated the procedure, stopping in the master bedroom—also empty.

Lir pulled out his dreaded cell phone and blinked at the screen. "Call Alex!" he commanded.

"Call Ambulance?" the robot voice asked.

"No, call Alex!" he repeated slowly.

"I do not understand, all calix."

He nearly screamed with anger. Instead, he muttered, "Motherfucker," and crushed his phone in his fist. Little bits of plastic, glass, and metal crumbled up in his hand. He shook it off, letting the pieces fall to the dingy carpet. He didn't feel sorry. "Good riddance."

"Um, boss? You know you can just touch the screen, right? You don't have to use voice command," Finn said, trying to be helpful.

"Call Alex," he demanded.

Finn cocked a grin. "Say please."

Lir locked eyes with him, one eyebrow up in warning. Finn said nothing, pulled out his phone, and called Alex.

"Tell him the house is clear," Lir said. "He and Jari can enter now."

Finn repeated the message, and a minute later, the pair joined them in the master bedroom.

"Something is off about this," Jari said as she paced the floor. "If Hecate found him here, he should be here. She used blood to call him. He has to be here."

Alex leaned against a wall and crossed his legs and arms. "He must be using magic. If we could get Hecate to wake the fuck up, she could help."

Finn delicately stroked Hecate's face. "Wake up, beautiful. We need you."

Hecate groaned and fluttered her eyelids. Then she leaned over and promptly threw up.

"Aw, damn. These are my favorite shoes," Finn sighed.

"I'll clean them later," Hecate muttered with a touch of irritation in her voice.

Lir couldn't blame her. She was the one who got sick, and Finn was worried about his shoes. He hurriedly told Hecate what was going on.

The witch closed her eyes for a moment. "His sorceress put a glamor spell in place. This house is a decoy, hiding his actual location. Most likely, he put this in place to hide from Zeus." She began walking around the room in a slow circle. "There." She pointed to the window. "See the faint shimmering? He is in another realm. This house is his anchor to the realm we are in. There should be an opening somewhere."

She walked around the house, muttering out loud like a crazy person as she ran her hands over the walls. It only took a minute or so before she spoke to the group. "Found it!"

Lir followed her voice and arrived at a closet. The door was an entryway to Olympus, also known as the Realm of the gods. The sweet perfume of his homeland wafted through the doorway. His stomach clenched in excitement. *Home!* Gods, he missed it. A slow smile spread across his face. He found himself filled with happiness. He looked around to his equally overjoyed comrades.

Perhaps with less caution than was prudent, they all fell through the portal, eager to visit home.

MYA

Mya stepped into the new world and sucked in a breath. This was the most amazing place she'd ever seen. The sky seemed to shine a brighter blue than the one on Earth, and even the air felt better. Cleaner, perhaps? And the smell . . . it was reminiscent of the most exquisite floral perfume one could buy. There were no words for the beauty she could see and feel. She felt she knew this place in her heart and soul. She had been here before; she just couldn't remember it.

"Where are we?" she asked in a breathy voice.

"Olympus," Lir replied. Reverence saturated his words.

"Wow."

"He hid in Olympus while pretending to hide on Earth. Genius," Jari said. Her head swiveled around to check out their surroundings.

"No one would expect him to hide here," Hecate agreed.

They stood in an airy great room. It had no roof and only Roman pillars for walls. Colorful birds perched on a willow tree in the middle of the room and chirped into the air. A variety of colorful cushions decorated the base of the tree. Branches anchored the sides of the cushions, fashioning them into chairs.

The group headed down the hallway. The floor sparkled with golden marble, and each of their heels made a clicking sound on it, announcing their presence.

They found Aiden in what Mya assumed was his bedroom. The king-sized, four-poster bed matched the chairs fashioned by the willow branches. They twisted together to form a canopy of sorts. Wildflowers grew all around it. The walls had open windows shaped like domes, reminding her of a picture she'd seen of Greece. A beautiful turquoise ocean filled the background, invading her senses with the scent of salt. Mya would give anything to give up her life on Earth and never leave this place.

A strange man stood in the corner, reclining against the wall with his arms over his chest. "The mighty Guardians have found me!" He grinned with a deranged tilt of his head. "I've been wondering when you'd get here. I knew you were coming, you see. You need me for your war." He paused. "Or did that already happen?" His face twisted into a thoughtful expression.

Just as she expected, he was beautiful. It hurt to gaze at him for too long. He was tall, broad, and well-muscled. His fierce brown eyes screamed of intelligence and his face belonged in a renaissance painting. The only things marring his beautiful exterior were the flaming red mohawk and the piercings lining his ears. She chuckled at the stark contrast. He appeared stuck in another era, something the gods seem to be fond of doing. They tried to fit in with normal culture but always seemed to fail just a bit.

Lir walked toward him. "Greetings, Aiden. The war has not yet happened, but it will. Zeus has already declared war on the humans, and he's threatened us to stay out of it. We've come to ask for your aid." He gave Aiden a pointed look. "Though, we won't force you."

Aiden leaned his head back, laughing as he sank onto the edge of his bed. It was a bitter, angry sound. He wouldn't be helping them. He was madder than hell, and was he drunk? Mya had been so busy staring at him, she hadn't noticed the various liquor bottles littering the floor.

"Why should I care what the hell Zeus does?" Aiden said when he finished laughing. "Or what he does to the humans?"

Lir stepped closer. "You always helped the humans in the past, even at the expense of your own well-being. Why did you change your mind? What happened to make you bitter and drunk, old friend?"

"I was tortured for centuries for those humans," he muttered. "Tortured!" He spoke louder this time and stood again, wobbly from the liquor. "They can die, for all I care. All of you go die, and let me drink in peace! I'll be joining you in death soon enough. I think?" His words slurred.

"Aiden. Don't do this. Don't let what happened to you turn you away from the mortals. They need you. If we don't help, everyone will die," Lir pleaded.

"I don't care." Aiden crossed his arms.

Alex spoke up from his perch on the end of the bed, his voice angry. "Then don't do it for the humans. Do it for yourself. Make Zeus pay for what he did to you! Let him scream, let him burn, and claim your vengeance!"

"I can't! Don't you see?" Aiden's voice cracked. "I'm not strong enough to defeat him." He fell onto his bed, curled into a ball, and started sobbing.

Jari climbed into the bed and cradled him, and they all sat in silence as he cried. Mya couldn't imagine being tortured for centuries. How broken he must be. She hated to admit it, but he wouldn't be helpful. Not like this. His mind was shattered.

Jari spoke to him softly. "We're trying to find all the allies we can. We need to stop him. I know you feel weak. Trust me, I know." Her voice broke off at the end. "You're angry, and you're hurting, but you need to do this. Forget about us, the humans, all of it. Think about you. *You* need to do this. *You* need to heal and move on. Together, we can stop him. We can help you, and you can help us." She stood and held her hand out to him. "Come on. Join us."

He lay there on the bed, his sorrow and grief lining every inch of his face. He looked around in a daze and stopped as he spotted Mya. His eyes cleared for a moment. "goddess, it can't be. Nyx?"

"No. My name is Mya. Nyx died, and I guess she's my soul or something like that." She felt unsure as she said it. She still had no powers and didn't feel like a goddess. Claiming that title felt false.

"We're helping Mya to access her goddess powers. Once we do, she'll be the strongest of us all." Jari looked at her, smiling with hope.

Aiden released a sigh. "If I'm to die anyway, I might as well go out with a bang, doing what's right. You're right, Jari. Look at me. I'm a broken, drunken mess. I need to heal myself." He hugged her tightly. "Come. I need to eat and sober up." Aiden stood and gestured for them to follow. "Make yourselves comfortable and rest."

He led them into an outdoor kitchen and started pulling out food. He filled a platter with fruit, crackers, meats, and cheeses. Mya was suddenly very hungry and remembered she wasn't able to eat earlier. It was funny how all the anxiety and weariness seemed to leave her when she entered the godly realm.

Aiden took a few bites, and around a mouthful of food, he said, "Talk. Tell me what's going on. I've been holed up here for so long, I've lost count of the years. I no longer know what is the past and what is the future." He looked up at the sky, thinking.

CHAPTER TWENTY-THREE

MYA

They all sat around, eating, talking, and catching Aiden up on the latest events.

"So, what's our next move? We try to break this curse first, or we meet the witches and unlock Mya's powers?" Aiden looked up and closed his eyes.

What is he doing?

They stood around in uncomfortable silence. Not knowing what to say to Aiden or whether they should interrupt whatever the hell it was he was doing.

Finally, he opened his eyes and spoke. "There are multiple outcomes. Too many to choose the correct course. In many outcomes, we all die, and Zeus prevails. In some, many will die, and Zeus will fail." He spread his arms wide as if to show how many courses there were. "There will be death, regardless. I'm too out of touch with my powers and need practice, but I think . . ." He paused and looked around the room. "I'm not sure, but I think we need to unleash Mya's powers before we do anything else." He brought his gaze to

Mya and stared at her with intensity. "She is the key—the catalyst, if you will. She decides our fate. She must be ready to embrace who she is and not run away in fear." He gave everyone a moment to take in his statement before finishing. "I suspect she doesn't feel comfortable as a goddess and isn't ready to join our cause. We must change that." He continued to stare her down, his eyes piercing into her soul.

He knew everything she was feeling, and that unnerved her. She wanted to run away. She wasn't a goddess. She didn't *feel* like a goddess. She wasn't strong like them, she didn't have access to any powers, and she didn't know the first thing about unlocking them. Her fighting skills weren't good enough, and she wasn't as beautiful as the others. The list could go on forever with all the ways she wasn't one of them. Why did they all have such faith in her?

She stared back into Aiden's soul-scorching eyes. "You're right. Everything you said is how I feel, but I'll try to stick with you guys for now." She looked around. Did they believe that she would try? Did she believe herself?

Jari smiled at her. "Give us time. Let us show you who you are and how to access your powers. I know you're strong. Nyx was one of the strongest. Zeus himself was wary of her powers, and you'll be just as strong. I know it."

She didn't have that same faith in herself, but she cared for these people and didn't want to let them down. But if the fate of humanity lay with trusting in herself, she wasn't too confident of the outcome.

The Guardians stood to leave, ready to get back to the safe house. The cool night air greeted them as they stepped outside. Mya inhaled the sweet, flowery scent one more time, saving it for her memories. She wouldn't soon forget this place, and hopefully, she'd be back one day.

Aiden had sobered up while packing an excessive amount

of stuff. The god seemed hell-bent on taking his entire library of books as well as his vast arsenal of weaponry. When it came time to lug those things through the portal, Mya would be hiding in a corner. No way was she volunteering for *that* duty.

As they readied to leave, an eerie, disembodied laugh joined the air. It stiffened Mya's spine, spiking fear deep in her core. She knew that laugh. Those horrid demons were here. With great effort, she steadied her breathing, keeping her limbs relaxed and steady. She would not show fear. Not again. This time, she had the Guardians, and protection was what they excelled at.

Lir growled angrily. The twang of steel rang out in the air as he released his sword. "Beelzebub's demons! Get back in the house!" Lir yelled.

They bolted back inside and barred the door.

Finn spun his ax around. "There aren't demons in Olympus. How did they get here?"

"Zeus must have granted them access." Lir's voice was filled with anger, and his scowl matched his tone.

Jari cursed as she checked her weapons. "He knows we're here."

"Damn. I timed it too late," Aiden muttered.

They all turned their attention to him.

"What do you mean, you timed it too late?" Lir asked in a calm voice.

Aiden tapped his head. "God of forethought, though my powers extend far beyond that. I can see the future . . . usually. I knew they would try to ambush us, but I thought I timed it correctly by stalling and slowly packing. Seems I thought wrong."

"Wouldn't it have made more sense to leave early?" Mya asked.

"Yes, it would have, but my mind is often confused these days." Aiden shrugged in apology.

Alex huffed. "Great. We found a god who cries like a girl and doesn't understand his powers anymore. How fucking useful."

"There's nothing wrong with a man who cries," Mya chastised. She didn't correct him on the powers comment, though. That *was* a problem.

"Men are often the biggest cowards," Hecate chided while slumped on a cushion. "I am far too weak to be of assistance. I'd rather not endanger anyone else, so I'll stay right here and conserve my strength."

Alex grunted at both women, clearly not agreeing with either comment.

Lir's commanding voice cut into the tension. "While you two are having a debate about men who cry, the rest of us are assessing the situation. Care to join the party, or should I just let the demons eat you?"

"These demons are vastly inferior," Alex said. "No assessment needed. We kill them."

Lir pointed at Mya. "We have to protect her. She can't fight yet."

Alex threw up a hand and gestured at her as well. "I've been teaching her to fight. She's not terrible."

Gee, that's reassuring.

"Still, we protect her." Lir looked at Aiden next and pointed to the door. "Is that the only way out?"

"I have an exit in the back that lets onto the beach." Aiden motioned toward somewhere behind him.

"Good," Lir said. "Jari and Alex, you're our best clandestine killers. Sneak out the back and circle around. Hide in the dark until we need you."

They looked at each other.

"Alex, you can climb in the trees and shoot them with your arrows," Lir continued. "Since the demons hide until just before they attack, try to spot any movement or disturbance and strike first."

They both nodded and took off.

Lir looked at Aiden again. "Does your fire work on demons?"

Aiden shook his head. "No. Doesn't even faze them."

"How are you with weapons?" Lir asked.

Aiden whipped out a sword, seemingly from nowhere. "As good as the rest of you. I can hold my own."

Lir nodded and directed his attention to Mya. "You stay behind the three of us at all times. We'll create a semi-circle around you, got it?"

"Yes." His insistence that she shouldn't fight grated against her nerves, but she was truly afraid of those demons.

"If one gets past us, you fight." He handed her a dagger. "Can you use this?"

She grabbed the dagger with trembling fingers and nodded hesitantly. "Alex taught me a little bit. I think I can handle it."

Lir nodded again and hugged her tightly. He was solid and warm in her arms. Normally, she hated hugging, but found this one wasn't entirely unwelcome.

"Good girl," he kissed her forehead. "We'll protect you, and if we can't, you'll protect yourself. I believe in you."

Everyone was having way too much faith in her today. She nodded along anyway.

Lir opened the door, and they all spilled out into the night. That same creepy laugh floated through the air. Mya cringed.

Be brave. Be brave! she chanted to herself.

An arrow zipped through the air so fast she barely saw it. It landed true. The demon's body appeared, lying on the ground, blood spurting out of its chest. Another body landed beside the first, its limbs chopped off. Mya thought she spotted Jari moving away from it.

Finn battled two demons. His movements were brutal but efficient. A kick to the head, flying fists, head-butting—he obviously wasn't afraid to fight dirty. His ax landed in the gut of a demon. He ripped it out, black gore dripping from the wedge-shaped blade. Without pause, he hacked his axe into the neck of the demon next to him. Both his demons were down.

Aiden battled multiple demons. He was just as efficient as Finn, but his motions were beautiful. A dance of death. He moved his sword like one would move an arm. Every strike was a kill strike. He struck one in the chest, shoved it off his blade, blocked a claw, and stabbed that one in the neck. Another demon swung toward him. Aiden ducked and thrust his sword up into the demon's thigh. A fountain of black goo sprayed onto him. He slid across the ground, slicing another demon behind the knees. It fell onto its face, and Aiden stabbed down, angling his sword into its neck.

Lir's fighting style was a mix of grace and brutality. He exuded confidence while wielding his sword. He swung it effortlessly, the blade moving in swirls of menace. He seemed particularly fond of cutting off heads. He stabbed one in the arm, swung around to kick another, and ended his kills with a nice, clean swipe through the neck. Demons fell at his feet quicker than Mya could count them.

They were winning. She wouldn't even have to fight!

The ground shook beneath her feet, followed by a great roar that could only belong to a massive beast. Despair and hopelessness washed away all hope that they would win this battle. She could sense the sheer size of this creature, and it terrified her.

A great black maw greeted them. Large canine teeth revealed themselves as the great beast let out another roar, shaking her to her very bones. Red eyes blazed into her core.

"What the fuck is that thing?" she shrieked.

A male voice answered, though Mya couldn't tell who it belonged to. "Demon dog! Let's hope there's only one."

Oh god, there could be more than one?

The ground shook again.

Fuck, there's more than one!

An arrow flew, landing in the dog's eye. The beast proved itself to be more than a dumb animal as it let out another great roar and pried the arrow out with a paw.

She heard Alex's voice from the trees. "Fuck me! Die, you bastard!"

Arrows zinged through the air, every one of them landing in the beast. It didn't falter; it didn't even remove the arrows this time. Instead, the demon dog reared its head back and howled, calling the other dogs to him.

Ten beasts announced themselves, growling and howling along with the first dog. Massive pools of drool landed in a puddle beneath them.

Lir whistled and ran toward the ocean, faster than lightning. He made a hand gesture, but Mya wasn't sure if he meant for her to follow or stay back. She looked to Aiden for help, and he shrugged.

She turned to Finn. "Do we follow him or stay here?"

"Um, I don't think he needs help if he's going to the ocean, but I guess we should be there. Follow him?"

"Follow him, you morons!" Alex shouted as he leaped from his perch in the tree. He landed on his feet and turned to Aiden. "Stay here with Mya and guard her."

"But I want to see what happens," she whined, and stomped her foot.

Alex stopped and thought for a moment. He sighed. "Fine, but if you die, I'm not taking the heat for it. I'll totally blame Aiden for letting you go since he's guarding you."

She grinned. She could live with that. "Deal. Let's go."

"Wait. What?" Aiden protested.

Not giving him time to stop her, she ran, silently thanking Alex for all his training. She was much faster than she ever had been.

They arrived on the beach. Even at night, it was beautiful here. The moonlight glittered off the soft waves created by the light breeze. The water turned into turmoil as great waves crashed into each other.

Mya's gaze was drawn up as she spotted Lir standing on the waves. He looked every inch the divine god he was. His raven hair had somehow grown and was now down to his waist, tinted in various shades of blue. The water glistened off his rippling muscles. Great black tentacles took the place of his legs, making him at least ten feet tall. He held a golden trident and seemed more at home with it than the sword he carried religiously.

The demon dogs splashed into the water, growling, roaring, and pawing at the sand. One lunged toward Lir's tentacles. He stabbed down into the beast with his trident, cleaving off the head. More dogs jumped and lunged at him. He stabbed one in the chest and threw it into the ocean. The waves washed it away to drown. He stabbed another through the neck, and that head rolled off too. The next two dogs were swallowed by the waves.

The water level rose, and with it came a great white shark. It caught a demon dog and tore into it with its many rows of pointed teeth, shaking it before spitting it out. The shark swam away as the wave receded. The canine was definitely dead.

Her attention was drawn to Lir as he raised his arms to the night sky, the water rising with him, catching the remaining demon dogs in its wake. Lir began twisting his arms in an intricate motion, his tattoos glowing blue and swirling along his arms. Both the sea and the dogs swirled into a tornado. It spun for a moment before crashing back down into waves, dragging the final four dogs out to sea.

The deed done, Lir shrank back to his human form and swam to the shore. He emerged from the water and walked to the beach, naked from head to toe.

What a beautiful sight, Mya thought dreamily.

Without stopping, he strolled back to Aiden's house. Mya watched his ass flex as he walked away.

"You got some clothes I can borrow?" he called out to Aiden.

She glanced over and noticed Aiden picking his jaw up off the floor as well.

Oh, good. I'm not the only one in shock at Lir's prowess.

"Yep. Help yourself," Aiden answered.

"Is the threat gone? Any more surprises?" Jari asked Aiden, waving her katana in his face like a lunatic.

"No. I think the threat is over now," Aiden said while looking up at the sky again.

This god is so weird.

Alex paused from collecting his arrows and snorted. "You think? Wonderful."

Aiden didn't answer him.

CHAPTER TWENTY-FOUR

MYA

Lir shrugged into a too-tight t-shirt and ordered everyone around as they prepared to leave. Finn and Aiden hefted the boxes of books while Alex and Lir grabbed the weapons cache. Jari helped with the clothing. Mya, miraculously, had nothing. She followed them through the portal and braced herself for the familiar feeling of falling. She checked her balance and landed in the living room on her feet this time.

Not bad, Mya, she thought to herself.

Lir was sitting on the couch, already comfortable. His arm rested against the sofa cushion, and his legs were sprawled out. "Zeus is watching us. He has to be." He was speaking to everyone. "That attack was planned perfectly. We need to stay at the safe house as often as possible and only leave when needed. Eventually, Zeus will realize we survived, and then he'll attack."

"The idiot should've attacked us on Terra, not in Olympus," Alex said, "and next to the ocean, no less."

"Let's be thankful for the oversight. We may not get another one," Jari added.

"Zeus is a fickle bastard who has no concept of time. He probably won't plan another attack for a long while. It'll take just as long for him to notice we killed his little pets," Alex said.

"Why demon dogs, though? Who could have aligned with him that has control of demon dogs? I doubt Hades would aid him." Jari was thinking out loud.

Alex flopped down on the couch. "No, Hades hates Zeus almost as much as he enjoys playing with the humans. They're too much fun for him, and if they all die, they won't stay in the underworld for long. He won't let Zeus take that away."

"Are we asking Hades to join us?" Mya asked with a quiver in her voice.

They stared at her like she'd swallowed a bug.

Jari broke the awkward moment. "We wouldn't dare ask *him* for aid. He's just as likely to murder us for the hell of it. We let him come to us, or we avoid him altogether."

Mya blew out a breath. "Good to know. I mean, I'm getting comfortable hanging out with gods and all, but I am so not ready to meet the god of death."

They all nodded their assent.

A voice whispered in the back of her head. *Erebus. Demon dogs. Erebus.* Was Nyx speaking to her? She figured it was worth mentioning. "Is it possible that Erebus controls the demon dogs?"

They considered her for a moment.

Aiden answered her. "Yes. I think it is possible he could have sent them. Perhaps Zeus knows about you and is using you to gain his help. I can't tell."

"Did you foresee the demon dogs?" Mya questioned.

Aiden shook his head. "No, whoever sent them was undecided until the last moment."

Hecate joined them in the living room, wearing her usual weird clothing. Her cat nightgown stood out amongst the sea of black leather. Her pet snake coiled around her neck and hung off the sides of her body.

Lir pointed to the snake. "I said no snakes in the house."

Hecate pouted her lips. "Fine." She walked to the front door, making sure to brush both her body and the body of her spirit against Alex. Forever taunting him.

He scowled in response but said nothing.

Lir caught Hecate up on the night's events since she'd been resting during the battle.

"I already warded this place. We should be fine until our next move," Hecate said with confidence.

Lir nodded. "Good. What of the curse? Were you able to access your memories?"

Hecate frowned. "No. Unfortunately, I cannot remember. It has been too long since the curse was placed. We will need to travel the river of Mnemosyne."

"What is the river of Mnemosyne?" Mya asked.

"A river that travels in the underworld, created by the goddess of memory. If one drinks from the river, they are said to be able to remember things that have been long forgotten," Hecate sounded almost dreamy.

"And if someone drinks from the parallel river of Lithe," Aiden said, "they will then forget their memories." Aiden looked at no one in particular as he spoke. He'd taken on the same dreamy tone as Hecate. "It is said, souls must drink from the river before they are reincarnated. I suspect if Mya drinks from the river, she may remember being Nyx. Which could be a bad thing." He shook his head. "To unleash several lifetimes of memory on one person can be dangerous."

Hecate nodded. "Agreed. It is better for her to learn her powers on her own and create her own memories." She shot a pointed look at Mya. "You must not drink from the river."

Mya nodded hastily. "Understood. I don't want those memories anyway."

Hecate smiled at her and turned to Lir. "We should wait to travel to the underworld until we have found the witches and unlocked Mya's powers. Once she has them, she will be more comfortable traveling in that place."

"Agreed," Lir said. "Do you still wield the keys to unlock the gates?"

"I do." Her spirit forms came to float behind her.

Lir smiled. "Excellent. We'll plan our travels as soon as the witch's ritual is over."

Alex snorted in disdain. "I am not traveling to the underworld with Hecate."

"You certainly will," Lir said. "We need her to unlock the gates and guide us, and I need you to help fight should we run into problems."

"These days, problems are guaranteed," Jari muttered.

Alex grumbled but didn't object. He knew Lir was right; they were both needed.

Aiden laughed and pointed between Alex and Hecate. "Funny how you two seem to hate each other."

Alex furrowed his brow. "Why is that funny?"

"Oh, you won't believe me." Aiden was giggling now.

"Humor me," Alex said, his tone blunt.

Aiden made some interesting gestures with his hands. "I saw a vision of the two of you quite . . . comfortable together. Perhaps in bed? Maybe moving around a bit . . ."

"What?" Alex and Hecate said in unison, for once in agreement.

"I said you wouldn't believe me," Aiden sang.

Alex and Hecate scowled at him.

Mya stood up. "Well, I'm beat. I'm going to bed while I still can." She started to walk away.

Lir called out to her. "Don't think I forgot about you ignoring my orders back there. I told you to stay put for your own well-being. Following the demon dogs was dangerous."

She'd had just about enough of being treated like a baby and getting bossed around. "Goodnight," she answered, and shut the bedroom door behind her.

৩৯৩

IT WAS ANOTHER TRAINING DAY, and Alex was barking orders per usual. "Move your feet!"

Oh, right. Mya looked down, focusing on moving her feet as she tried to wield her overly heavy sword. "Ouch!" she cried out, nearly dropping her sword. Again.

"Never look away from your opponent!" Alex scolded.

"Did you have to stab me, though? Why the hell are we using real swords, anyway?" Mya touched her side gingerly, wiping away the blood.

"Quit being such a girl! It's just a stab wound. You're an immortal goddess. Act like it!"

"I'm a girl, and stab wounds hurt. Especially for someone who's never been stabbed before!" Mya continued clutching her side.

He gave her a wry smile. "Should I keep stabbing you? You know, for practice?"

"No!"

"Then stop pouting and lift your sword!"

With a tinge of regret, she let go of her side and raised her sword, bending her knees in what she thought was the correct attack stance.

"Not like that. Gods! How many times must I show you how to hold your damn sword?"

She whined and dropped her arms. "It's heavy and awkward, and I'm short, and my arms hurt!"

Alex frowned. "Get used to it. Practice, practice, practice. Eventually, your sword will feel like an extension of yourself, and you won't feel comfortable without it."

"Do I have to use a sword? Can't I try something else, like a gun? Yes, a gun! I like guns," she said.

"Guns don't work on most immortal beings or monsters. You must start with a sword first. You must learn the basics before we branch out and try other weapons. Furthermore, the sword I gave you is lightweight, small, and easy to use for beginners."

If this sword was lightweight, she didn't want to use any other sword. Ever.

"Fine. I'll use this sword and practice, but can't we at least take breaks." She pouted, looking up at him and begging with her eyes.

"Do you think your enemy will give you a break because you're tired? *Hmm?"*

She scowled at him and swung her sword toward his head, hoping to hit home and give him a little "stab wound." He lazily blocked it with his blade and shoved her back ten feet. Her feet scraped against the ground as she scrambled for purchase, fighting to stay upright.

"Do you have to be so strong, you bastard?" She gritted her teeth.

He chuckled a bit. "Many of your enemies will be stronger than you. You must practice with that thought in mind. You must be faster. Get in close to your enemies and always protect your body."

Mya tried to shove him off with a push of her sword but

failed. She kicked him, and her foot met with hard, unyielding muscle. The impact reverberated through her leg, and her bones vibrated with the force of it.

"Ow, ow, ow!" She grabbed her leg and started rubbing out the aches. "Please give me a break now. I think I broke something kicking you." She knew how childish she sounded, but she didn't care.

"Suck it up, you whiny bitch," Alex said with a menacing look.

Whiny bitch? I'll show you whiny bitch, she thought.

She feigned weakness, allowing him to come toward her with the sword. He bent down, taking away his height advantage. Once he was close, she raised her sword and swiped toward his ribs. She jumped up and down with satisfaction when she spotted blood trickling from his side.

"Yes! Ha! I stabbed you back," she said, grinning. "Who's the whiny bitch now?"

He responded by drop-kicking her, and she hit the ground hard.

Goddammit!

"You stabbed me. Yes, good job. But you let your guard down. You must wait until your opponent is down before you celebrate your victory." He reached down and hauled her back onto her feet.

"Again!" He raised his sword and swung.

She blocked, aimed, and swung again, trying to remember her footwork as they danced around. Her muscles burned and ached with fatigue. Despite all the work she put forth during her workouts and training, she was still too weak—but she was getting stronger.

Lir stepped out of the house, striding toward them on powerful legs. "I can't watch this anymore. You need to train harder. How are you going to fight a god when you can't even hold your sword?"

Mya blew out a breath and dropped her weapon. It fell to the ground with a clang. "Alex is training me just fine. We don't need you."

"Oh really? Pick up your sword," Lir said.

She raised one brow. "Why?"

"Just fucking do it." Lir pulled out his own sword from the sheath he always wore strapped to his back, though he usually wore a suit shirt over it. Today, he wore gym shorts and a tank that highlighted every delicious aspect of his arms.

"Fine." She huffed and bent down to retrieve her sword.

She'd barely slipped her fingers over the cool metal before Lir swung his sword in her direction. The blade whizzed through the air in a nearly indistinguishable blur.

Mya fumbled with the sword and blocked the attack. The force of the clashing weaponry sent vibrations down her arms. Her blade was the only thing separating Lir's sword from her face. Her eyes widened in surprise. She hadn't realized it had come that close to cutting her.

She scowled at him. "What the hell? Are you trying to kill me?"

"You can't die. You're a goddess, and it's time you learned to fight like one. Alex is being too kind. Get up! Now!"

Mya scrambled to her feet, scraping the sword across the ground. "I hate you!" She spat at his feet.

"I can live with that." He swung his blade down toward her in another flash of movement.

She dodged to the right and swung. Lir stepped over the blade. She'd aimed for his ankles or the back of his knees, just as Alex had taught her. His words flashed through her mind. *You are smaller and weaker, so always try to maim your opponent as fast as possible.*

She lunged, ready to strike again. Her sweat-soaked hands slipped down the pommel of the sword. It fell from her grip and slid across the ground.

Lir paused his onslaught and lowered his sword. "Hold."

He stepped closer, invading her space with his radiant heat and the scent of the ocean. Her heart raced against her ribcage. The closeness reminded her of her lustful dreams starring the god of the sea. His eyes bored into hers as he inched even closer, his lips parted.

She swallowed. "W-what?"

Lir reached down, placing his large, rough hands over hers. "Let me show you how to hold your sword properly." He moved her grip, placing one hand below the hilt and the other on the pommel. Next, he adjusted her fingers and angled her wrists. "There. Does that feel more comfortable?"

She nodded, not trusting her voice.

"Good."

He eased behind her, and she could feel every hardened inch of him against her. Her thoughts muddled together, and her ears buzzed.

Once again, he wrapped his hands over hers, raised both their arms together, and swung the blade through the air. "See how much easier it is to weild your weapon when your hands are in the right position?"

Her eyes met his, and she stared into the swirling orbs. His lips moved closer to hers . . . so close . . . then he shook his head, backed up, and walked in front of her, giving her a wide berth. She blew out air. Her mind cleared, and her heart slowed. She was thankful one of them had walked away before things got serious.

"Again," Lir commanded, his voice rough and thick.

Mya checked the position of her hands, readied her stance, and swung. The blade arced low. Lir deflected it with his sword and pushed. She stumbled back, her feet scraping against the ground. Again.

Lir released his hold on his sword, causing her to trip and fall forward. She rolled to stand, only Lir was already swinging his weapon. She shrieked, dropped her blade, and covered her head.

I'm gonna die. I'm gonna die. I'm gonna die.

Lir's sword thudded to the ground. She flinched, slowly lowering her arms as she peeked up at him. He stood over her, sweat dripping down his face, chest heaving, and a scowl painted on his lips.

"Get up." He offered her his hand.

She grasped it, feeling his warmth radiating through her palm.

He pulled her to her feet and took her chin between his thumb and finger. "Do not ever fear me. I will never intentionally harm you. I only want you to train harder."

She nodded, too afraid to speak, though she wasn't sure she believed him. He'd been swinging that sword pretty hard and fast.

Alex stepped forward from his position against a tree. He smiled maniacally, clapping his hands. "Bravo, you trained her so well."

Lir scowled. "You know I hate sarcasm."

"Bully for you. I'm the king of sarcasm." He clasped his hand on Lir's shoulder. "Now you know why I've been training her too . . . *kind,* as you called it. So how about you let me do my job from now on and you do yours? Unless you want her to hate you more than she already does."

Lir grimaced. "Point made." He lit a cigarette and walked back toward the house.

Mya blew out a breath and took a step forward. Alex blocked her with his sword.

"Oh, come on. I'm tired!" she said.

"Never drop your weapon. Pick it up and carry it with you always."

She sighed and picked up her sword. Alex relented and followed her toward the house.

Jari met Mya just outside the safe house. "Alex driving you crazy, or is it Lir?" she whispered.

"Both."

Jari giggled. "I thought so. You look tired and annoyed."

Gee, I love being told I look tired.

"Alex means well," Jari said. "He wants you to be the best and believes you have what it takes. It's a compliment to be trained by him, really." She guided Mya into the house.

"I suppose you're right," Mya said, "though I don't feel like agreeing right now."

"You just need some food and rest, and you'll be good as new. Plus, this time tomorrow, you might have access to your powers. Then I *guarantee* you'll put Alex in his place." Jari spoke with an air of confidence Mya couldn't understand.

She'd been avoiding thoughts about releasing her powers, too afraid the Guardians had mixed her up with someone else and would send her back to her despondent life once they realized it. She was starting to like them. All of them. If she had to leave, she would miss them very much.

A spicy aroma greeted her as she walked into the kitchen. Lir stood at the counter, cutting up food. He was still sweaty from their training session, but he at least looked calmer. A large pot rested on the stove. Mya had noticed that Lir liked to cook when he was stressed, which meant he cooked a lot. She wasn't about to complain, though. The meals alone were enough of a reason to want to stay with the Guardians.

Lir didn't spare them a glance as he started barking orders. "Get cleaned up and gear up. We leave after dinner." He didn't glance back to see if they would listen. He knew they would.

"You can kiss my ass," Alex muttered, but he didn't stop to object further.

Something about Lir's orders made you want to listen, no matter how sensible or how deplorable. Still, Mya tried to fight him whenever she could, just off principle. No one was telling this girl what to do.

CHAPTER TWENTY-FIVE

MYA

After getting cleaned up and strapping on her sword and gun, Mya headed to the dining room for dinner. Finn and Jari sat next to each other, both wearing the weapons and leather gear they were so fond of. They were currently fighting over a bread roll.

"I touched it first. Let go!" Finn growled as he tried to wrench the roll from Jari's iron grip.

Jari scoffed. "You already had three of them! Let. *Go!*"

Lir slammed a basket on the table, the force causing a resounding crack. He must have broken the basket somehow. "I made more, ingrates."

Finn released the roll, scooped up a handful of the fresh ones, and deposited them on his plate with glee. Mya stifled a laugh. There was no room for humor tonight. Her insides were doing flips in anticipation of today's events. She wasn't sure if her stomach would tolerate dinner or promptly expel it.

She chose a seat next to her new best friend, Alex, who

was currently frowning at Hecate as if she'd somehow poisoned his dinner. Lir was at the head of the table like the king he felt he was, and Aiden was at the other end, liberally pouring a bottle of vodka into his cup.

Why bother?

The oak dining table for eight was starting to feel too small for their ever-growing party.

"The witches will all be there," Lir said. "I went to the location by portal and scouted the area. They were oblivious to any danger and have likely warded the park anyway. We'll travel by car to avoid Zeus and any spies. Some of them monitor the portals."

Yay, no portal travel.

The rest of the table groaned.

"Driving is so boring," Finn complained around a mouthful of food, which was slightly disgusting.

Lir rolled his eyes. "We're not driving cross-country. You can handle it."

Alex continued looking at Hecate and asked, "Are we *all* going in a car together?"

Lir stopped cutting into his food. "Yes. We may need all of us, especially Hecate."

Alex sniffed at his food.

"If I poisoned your food," Hecate said, "you wouldn't be able to smell it or taste it." She tossed a black lock of curls behind her shoulder.

Alex pushed away his plate, deciding not to eat.

"She didn't touch your food, Alex. I made it," Lir said.

"Besides, if I decide to kill you or torture you, it'll be by my own hand, not garlic potatoes." Hecate smiled wickedly, enjoying her teasing. Or maybe she was serious. Mya could never quite tell.

"As if you would be able to," Alex grumbled. He pulled his plate back and started eating.

Hecate leaned forward slightly and opened her mouth to mess with Alex once more.

"Hecate," Lir warned.

She leaned back and started eating.

How the hell did he do that? Mya noticed one of Hecate's spirit forms lingering behind Alex and suppressed a smile.

Aiden giggled in the background.

"What is so funny, drunk man?" Alex asked.

"Oh no, I will be keeping *that* vision to myself." He hiccuped.

"How can you even get visions when you're drunk?" Finn asked, again with food in his mouth.

Yuck.

"I get visions just fine all the time. In fact, being drunk just makes them more manageable. The problem is that sober me doesn't remember the visions drunk me had." He giggled again.

"Wonderful," someone said dryly.

"Eat your food and get sober. We need you," Lir demanded with a scowl. He finished eating and excused himself to smoke a cigarette.

They all wrapped up and joined him outside to find a big black SUV equipped with a third row, bulletproof glass, and armored siding.

Are we going to war? Geez, talk about overkill.

"I call front!" Finn and Jari said simultaneously. They scrambled over each other to get to the car, just like kids.

Mya was starting to understand Lir's smoking habit.

"You're both getting in the back. Alex gets the front because he's the biggest," Lir said, digging the keys out of his pocket.

"Hah!" Alex called out, and climbed into the front seat. He turned to Hecate. "If you sit behind me, it will not be pleasant for you."

Hecate looked as if she would do exactly that, just to see how Alex would respond. Before she could climb in, Lir stopped her and made her sit behind him. Mya slid into the furthest row with Jari and prepared for what would surely be a horrible hour, stuck in the car with a bunch of impatient gods who normally used a thirty-second portal to travel.

☙❧

THE GUARDIANS ARRIVED at Alki Beach and found the park where the witches had gathered. Lir parked the SUV behind some large trees, hiding it from sight. They all climbed out with a combined enthusiasm. Mya took the time to look around, enjoying the cool, salty breeze. She was starting to enjoy that scent very much.

Huge, hundred-foot oak trees adorned the park. The wet grass was greener than any she'd seen before, and the air was still damp from the recent rain. She was growing accustomed to the frequent Washington precipitation.

They strolled out, heading toward the congregation of witches. She could see them in the distance, dancing in the firelight . . . naked as the day they were born. Mya shouldn't have been surprised by that. It seemed like something witches would do.

A tall, willowy blond approached. Her breasts bounced as she walked toward the group of gods, causing Mya all sorts of discomfort. She wasn't attracted to women, yet she couldn't help staring.

Would it be too much for her to put some clothes on?

"Welcome, Guardians. We have been expecting you. My

name is Alice." She waved her arms toward the group of bare, dancing women. "This is our coven."

Finn stepped up and addressed her. Rather, her boobs, because that's where he was looking. "Hello, beautiful." He smiled at her in a way that made all women sigh.

Blushing red, the woman took his hand and led him to the rest of her coven.

"How did you know we were coming?" Finn asked her, still looking too far down.

Alice smiled. "Come now, Finn. You're smarter than that, or so it seems. We're witches, and many of us are gifted in prophecy. If that's not enough evidence for you, we knew who you were as soon as you tripped our wards." She stopped in front of the coven. "Let me introduce all of you."

She pointed to another tall, willowy, and blond woman. "This is my sister, Anna."

Alex covered his front discreetly, cleared his throat, and asked in a gruff voice, "Not that I'm complaining or anything —I love a naked woman as much as any man—but why are you all nude?"

Anna smiled as she looked him up and down. "It's called sky-clad. It means we are one with nature and closer to the gods." Her voice was light and musical. "Of course, we never dreamed of being *this* close to a god." She bit her lip.

Alex probably creamed his pants.

Next, they met a handful of women who all seemed to look alike with their blond heads, beauty, and willowy physique. Mya couldn't remember all their names.

One of the women waved them toward the altar. "Come! Join us as we celebrate. How lucky are we to be graced with the presence of the gods and goddesses on this day?"

Lir offered a gentle smile—something Mya had only seen on his face a few times.

"Actually," he said, "we don't have time to celebrate. We waited until nightfall so we wouldn't disrupt your festivities, but time is of the essence. I'm afraid we must ask for your help and be on our way."

Alice stuck out her bottom lip in a pout, something Mya knew she would look terrible doing, but Alice managed to make it look cute.

"I had hoped to celebrate with the gods, but we understand that you cannot," Alice said, and walked past the raging bonfire.

Aiden paused in front of it, studied it with a cocked head, and shot fire from his hands, causing the inferno to blaze higher. The witches bowed down to him, laying themselves at his feet.

"Thank you for your blessing, kind god."

Aiden, who was still drunk, staggered and snickered like a little girl. "It was easy, really. No problem." He helped one of the women back to her feet and didn't even bother to look at her face. He blatantly checked out her body, and she let him.

Mya, preoccupied by the sexual harassment in progress, didn't notice that their group had stopped walking. She bumped into Jari. "Oops, sorry," she whispered.

"You don't have to whisper," Jari said with a laugh.

"It's just this altar . . . the celebration . . . it seems so sacred, you know? Also, I don't want to bring any male attention our way. They're pretty excited right now."

"Ah, the real reason you're whispering." Jari laughed and cupped a hand around Mya's ear as she whispered back. "The car ride is going to be hell. The boys will be rubbing one out in the back seat."

Mya smacked Jari on the arm. *"Ew!"*

Jari chuckled and rubbed her arm in mock pain. Lir shot them a dirty look.

Alice waved her arm. "Here we are—the altar. We'll use this for the ritual."

Mya studied the birch wood altar. The branches twisted into each other. Flowers of all shapes, colors, and sizes curled around it protectively. At the foot of the altar lay a rug in vibrant greens and yellows, a sun threaded into the center.

Alice sat down in the middle of the rug, tailor fashion—a terrible idea for a naked woman—and held out her hands. "Come. Join me under the altar."

Mya sat, and the Guardians surrounded the rug in a circle.

Alice directed Mya in front of her and held out her hands, palms up. "Join your hands with mine," she said.

Hesitantly, Mya placed both her hands in Alice's, taking care to not visibly cringe, lest Alice think she was being rude. Unwelcome fingers probed inside Mya's mind, touching places they shouldn't. Revolted, she pushed back, blocking those fingers. They didn't belong inside her head. Sweat poured down her face, but she felt it distantly. She was locked inside her mind in a battle of wills as she fought to push out that unwanted presence. She imagined a brick wall behind her eyelids and fortified it until it was hard and unyielding.

A warm hand touched her shoulder, and Mya jolted, opening her lids. Jari stared at her with wide eyes.

"What did you do to her?" Jari pointed to the witch who was lying on the ground, panting heavily.

"Oh no! Did I do that? How? Is she okay?" The words spilled out faster than Mya could process them.

Anna answered her fervent plea. "She's okay. A battle of the minds can be a powerful thing, but she's a strong witch, and she should be just fine." Anna helped Alice back into a sitting position and offered her some water.

"You're very strong, but why did you push me out?" Alice asked with a soft smile.

"Because it felt wrong. I could feel your presence in my mind, and it didn't feel like it belonged there." Mya wasn't sure how else to explain that feeling.

"You're a private person," Alice said. "You guard your heart with bars of steel and don't open it for anything. That's why my presence felt unwelcome to you. But that is no way to live, child. That will only lead to a life of despair and loneliness. You must allow your heart to feel again."

Mya lifted her brow. "You got all that from my head, or from the fact that I didn't want you in my mind?"

Alice gave her a knowing smile. "Both. I'm an empath. I feel what other people feel. Their emotions, thoughts, and desires. As a seer, I can also read their past, present, and to some extent, their future."

Mya was stunned and wanted to roll away from this witch as far as she could go. She was starting to understand Alex's aversion to their kind. "Do you need to touch me to get all that information?"

Alice shook her head. "Of course not. The touch was to find the source of your power. You can't access your power until you open your heart and free it from its prison. You must allow yourself to feel again. That's the only way."

Mya couldn't do that. Could she? Could she allow herself to feel love again and care for another? Every person she'd opened her heart to had hurt her. Could she survive any more sorrow?

Alice's soft voice broke through her reverie. "Look around you, child. Look who guards and protects you. They ask nothing of you. They demand nothing. They only want you to be free and strong."

Mya looked around. Jari, her kindhearted friend, stood next to her with one hand on her shoulder and the other on her weapon. Finn stood behind Alice, axe ready to defend. Lir was directly behind her. She didn't need to see him to know that. She could feel his demanding presence and smell his scent—seawater and a hint of cigarettes. Alex stood a bit further away, locked in a warrior pose. Even Aiden and Hecate, whom Mya barely knew, were standing around, ready to aid her should something go amiss.

Alice was right. These Guardians cared for her. They had since the day she met them. Jari and Alex even became her friends, and Lir . . . well, he was *something* to her. Could she let him in? Could she love this man? *Should* she love him?

"There you go. I can already feel you letting them in. Open those steel bars of yours. Now we can get to work on unlocking your powers. I have a feeling they'll be marvelous." Alice smiled widely.

The witches gathered around the altar, forming a loose circle. They began brainstorming a way to release her abilities.

"A strong witch placed the barrier on her," Alice said. "I could feel it when I reached her mind, but I think we can break through if we all work together." She studied Mya the way a scientist would analyze a new virus.

Another witch crossed her arms and spoke in a meek voice that could barely be heard over the silence. "What if she can't control them? Her powers are strong. Her aura is one of the brightest and strongest I've ever seen . . ." Her voice trailed off at the end.

Alice continued staring at Mya with wide and creepy eyes. "I think the Guardians should be able to handle her if she loses control, because you're correct, Kate. She is power-ful. Good observation." Alice finally looked away and smiled at Kate.

Another witch stepped closer to Mya, reaching a hand toward her head. Mya scooted back.

Alex grabbed the witch by her hair and yanked her backward. "Too close," he grunted.

"*Ouch!*" the witch yelled as she gingerly stroked her head. "Was physical violence necessary, you brute?"

Alex shrugged, unconcerned. "It's my job to protect her."

One of the witches scoffed. "She doesn't need protection. Alice is the strongest in the coven, and Mya lay her flat on her back on the ground."

Alex turned his fierce eyes toward the witch. "In a mind battle, yes, she's strong, and her powers showed in that battle. Physically, she's not there . . . yet." He turned to Mya, as if remembering she still sat at the altar, on display like a turkey on Thanksgiving. "No offense," he added.

Mya wasn't offended. He was right. Physically, she still needed help. "None taken," she reassured him.

Alice positioned Mya in the center of the circle on her back. Lir hovered over her the way a mother watches her newborn baby.

"Remember that personal-space thing?" She reached out her hand and shoved him back.

He grimaced and backed up a half-inch. "Sorry."

Alice grabbed four witches and placed them strategically around Mya in the cardinal directions. She barked out orders, and the remaining witches scrambled to collect their supplies. She then turned her attention to the gods. "May I ask the mighty gods for assistance? The elemental powers you wield will help me break the spell. Normally, we use elemental witches." She gestured to the witches circling Mya. "I think the god powers will be a wonderful aid and will certainly be powerful enough to break the spell."

The gods nodded their consent, excluding Alex.

He studied Mya before speaking. "If she needs me, I'll assist, but leave me as a last resort."

Alice nodded to him respectfully as another witch handed her a golden chalice and an ancient-looking athame.

Witches and their artifacts. She kept that thought to herself. Angering Witches who were about to cast or break a spell on her didn't seem wise.

Alice turned to Hecate and bowed. "My lady, would you like to do the honors?"

Hecate smiled kindly. "I will be content to watch your coven work tonight."

Alice blushed and bowed again, apparently overwhelmed by what she thought was an enormous compliment. Mya suspected the real reason Hecate declined was that she didn't want to waste her precious time and effort.

Alice positioned Lir with the water witch, Finn with the Earth witch, and Aiden with the fire witch. She turned to Mya, knife in hand—the very picture of a serial killer. With a slash, she sliced into Mya's palm and poured her blood into the chalice.

Mya stifled a scream.

Alice walked toward Finn and his witch. "We call on the powers of the Earth. Hear my plea!"

The earth witch lit a bundle of branches as Finn plunged his hands into the ground, his eyes glowing green. The earth answered their plea, the ground shaking with power as the scent of freshly mown grass floated around them.

Alice turned to Lir and his witch, her voice louder this time. "We call on the powers of the sea! Hear my plea!"

The water witch poured out her chalice as Lir raised his arms and shot water into the sea from his fingertips. The sea answered, and the waves crashed against the beach violently.

Alice turned to Aiden and his witch, her voice a fervent cry. She was getting weaker. "We call on the powers of the volcano. Hear our plea!"

The fire witch lit a stack of twigs lying in front of her. Aiden pumped his fire into it. The flames roared, licking higher and higher. The smoke and smell of sulfur saturated the air.

Alice turned to Hecate, her face a ghostly white as she screamed, *"We call on the power of spirit! Hear our plea!"* She dumped the chalice of blood on the ground, circling Mya. A faint breeze raised Alice's hair and drifted toward Mya.

Testing her.

Did she deserve spirit?

Was she strong enough to handle it?

Hecate aided her. She cut her own palm with the Athame and sprinkled her blood on the ground, mixing it with Mya's. The air stopped its assessment and rose into a swirling tornado. Ghosts of all kinds sprouted from the ground.

Spirit had answered.

CHAPTER TWENTY-SIX

MYA

A lice sank to her knees beside Mya and raised her hands to the sky. One of the witches rose and handed her an ancient looking tome. The pages were not paper. The cover appeared to be made of some kind of skin. Odd, indecipherable symbols covered it. Alice stared at the page and started chanting.

"Ex luna scientia, esto quod es, ex animo lucter.
Et emergo fortis et liber!"

The other witches joined her in the chant,

"Ex luna scientia, esto quod es, ex animo lucter.
Et emergo, fortis et liber!"

A voice whispered in Mya's mind like a seductive caress. *Are you sure? Can you handle the powers of the night? The call of the moon? Can you?* The voice taunted her.

Mya answered in her mind. Her voice held no hint of fear. *Yes!*

Louder now, the witches chanted.

Mya felt the moon's power. She felt the stars. The night called to her.

If you are sure, the voice answered. It was no longer a caress or a whisper. It was now her own mind—her own voice—that spoke to her.

"*Ex luna scientia, esto quod es, ex animo lucter.*
Et emergo fortis et liber!"

Mya opened her eyes and stared in awe. The night was alive. She could feel its vast energy, and all of it was at her fingertips. She stretched her limbs, embracing her power. Her hair had grown the length of her body and was the color of darkness. Stars gleamed within her tresses. She shook her head in wonder and focused on the shadows surrounding her.

They danced around her, enticing her and stroking her body with love, as a cat would. She reached out an arm, and the shadows enveloped her, wrapping in tight coils around her. She should have been scared, but she wasn't. She felt comfortable and more like herself than ever before. How had she ever doubted herself?

She was powerful, just like the Guardians said she would be.

Oh, yes. Powerful.

She felt that vast power in her grasp and grew drunk on it. She could do anything. *Anything.* To hell with Zeus! She'd find every fucker who'd hurt her and make them pay.

Oh, yes. She would.

She'd find that ex-boyfriend in his bed and wrap her shadows around him. She'd watch him scream in fear as he tried to find light, any light, only to be suffocated by the dark. She would find her ex-best friend and do the same to her. She would find every foster parent who rejected her, and when she was finished, maybe she'd attack Zeus.

But did she want to?

Hell, Zeus was right! The humans didn't care for the gods. Even worse, the humans didn't care for each other. They treated each other horribly and should be eradicated. They *deserved* to be eradicated.

A scream tore through the air, startling her. Mya opened her eyes and looked up to see what the commotion was about. The moon and stars stared back at her, much too close. She looked down and found that she was floating—*levitating*—with her shadows wrapped around her body. She searched for the source of the scream and found nothing. Her shadows had obscured the park in a cloak of darkness.

Mya strained her eyes and tried to focus on where she thought the witches might be. The park lit up in color, momentarily blinding her. As her vision adjusted, she beheld a horrific sight. The shadows were strangling the witches, shrouding them in darkness.

Mya reached out a hand and released forth the power coiled inside her, commanding the shadows and calling them back to the night. They obeyed, slithering away from the coven. The witches echoed their relief.

What have I done?

The witches only wanted to help her, not hurt her. This was wrong. Hate and vengeance weren't the answers. She had to be more careful. This power was dangerous, and it was ruled by emotion. With that thought, she plunged to the ground.

Lir caught her in the air, cradling her. "Are you okay?" he asked, worry in his eyes.

She nodded, unable to form words. Gently, he placed her on wobbly legs, and she struggled to stand.

"Um, boss? We've got problems!" Jari yelled as she spun her weapons around in her hands.

Finn growled. "The Walking Dead rejects are here."

"The Vrykolakas," Lir growled, pulling out his sword.

Mya turned her attention to the source of discord. There, standing just a block away, was an army of redheads. Thousands of them were packed in like sardines. They seemed ordinary at first glance until she saw the swiftness of their movements and the fangs protruding from their mouths.

Lir stared them down, standing tall like a statue. He was so beautiful, so fierce, and so much a warrior. Mya wanted to jump his bones and ravage that beautiful body, feel that power and passion as he wrapped his arms around her . . . and then he spoke.

"Mya, stand behind me, do you understand?" He shoved her behind his massive body.

"No way!" She tried to push him away, but it was like trying to move a mountain. "I have my powers now. I'm not a baby. Quit protecting me!"

"You don't know how to use them yet!" he snapped back.

"I don't care. I'll figure it out. I'm one of you, a goddess, and this is my fight, too. I'm not leaving you without another fighter!" She crossed her arms in defiance.

He sent menacing fury in her direction. For a moment, she faltered, ready to give in to his demands before realizing that was madness. She wouldn't let him control her.

"You are, perhaps, the most important piece of the war," he said. "If you die now because you're not ready, what then? Hmm?"

She stared him down, matching his fury. "So the rest of you are expendable? Is that it?"

"Don't put words in my mouth!" he bellowed. "Think about it. If you die, we *all* die!"

"Or, I do what I'm meant to do, and I fight, causing us to win this battle," she countered. "Did you think about that?"

He held her gaze, unrelenting. It was a battle of wills as they eyed each other with equal stubbornness.

Alice's voice cut through their argument, interrupting the silence. "I put up a shield. It will hold them, but not for long." She turned to Hecate, who, of course, wasn't helping. "Can you help Mya? What of her powers? Do you know of her history?"

Hecate stared at the night sky before answering. "Nyx controlled shadows and dreams, caused day to become night, and could make someone fall asleep by touching them. She also used the powers of the moon somehow. That's all I have."

Mya turned to Lir. "Good enough for you, o majesty?" she asked dryly. She was in this fight. No more hiding like a coward.

"Fine. When you die, don't say I didn't warn you!" He turned his back to her, done with the conversation. He always had to have the last word.

Alex pulled out a gun, handed it to Mya without hesitation, and unsheathed his sword. "I always wanted to go to battle protecting witches," he said, sounding like he wanted to do anything but.

Missing the sarcasm, Anna swooned and seductively wrapped her arm around his. "I love a man who fights for me."

He shrugged her off. "Sorry, sugar. I wouldn't touch you if you were the last woman alive." He caught her pout and added, "No offense."

Anna stalked away in an outrage.

He looked at Mya. "I apologized, didn't I? That's what no offense means."

"Um . . . yeah." Deciding to help, Mya looked at Anna. "He's afraid of witches. It's nothing personal."

The witches all giggled and promptly shut up when Alex leveled them with a look.

Faintly, Mya heard the whispering voice of the quiet witch from earlier. "I thought he was a god?"

She stifled a laugh.

"I am a god!" Alex bellowed.

Despite his yelling, the witches were no longer paying attention to him. The Vrykolakas were closer now. Alice fell to her knees, face drawn, teeth gritted, and sweat pouring down her body. Holding the shield was sapping her strength, and she was fading fast.

"I've thought of several scenarios in my head," Aiden said, "and have found the best possible one, though it is hazy and unsure at best."

Lir scrubbed a hand down his face. "Very well. What do we need to do?"

"As soon as Alice loses her hold on the barrier—which will be at any moment—I'll burn them. My fire will take out about a couple hundred, but I'll be incapacitated afterward. I need your word, Lir, god of the sea, leader of the Guardians . . . if I take them out, I want protection."

Lir nodded his assent, and Aiden continued.

"Mya will then cloak them with her shadows and darkness. They'll be slightly vulnerable, giving us a small advantage to fight. You'll lead some of them to the sea, where you're stronger—"

Lir scoffed. "No shit, Sherlock."

"—and the rest of you will fight here," Aiden finished.

Alice lost hold of the barrier, falling face-first into the ground. Her coven circled around her protectively. Hecate disappeared, and Aiden positioned himself to fire. He shot out his hands, unleashing a torrent of flames and burning the monsters to a crisp. They didn't scream, either because they didn't feel pain, or the fire was too fast or hot.

Mya hurried to call forth the darkness and shadows, releasing them onto the creatures. Again, they didn't scream.

Jari lunged, both katanas raised high. "They don't feel pain!" she shouted before plunging her blades into the Vrykolakas on each side of her. In a deadly dance, she turned her attention to the rest of the horde.

Alex jumped into the foray with a battle scream, moving faster than light. Watching him in battle, Mya realized he'd held back in their sparring sessions. His motions were a blur. The Vrykolakas were just as fast, dodging his sword strikes. Alex countered this by kicking or punching at them, varying his attacks so they couldn't anticipate his next move.

Finn had his hands in the grass, his eyes glowing a luminescent green. The trees around the park followed his command, wrapping the creatures in vines and branches. Finn rounded them up and hacked into them with his ax. Their heads rolled off in sickeningly slow motion, and blood ran through the park in rivulets.

Mya looked for the witches. They were holding their own, chanting a spell. She had a sneaking suspicion it was an invisibility spell. She strained to keep an eye on everyone. The battle was moving so fast.

Lir used the sea to wrap the monsters in waves, washing them away. The creatures were smarter than they appeared, and they slowly backed up to fight on the beach, forcing Lir to join them.

Mya heard a scream. She looked at Finn and saw that he was bleeding heavily, growing weaker with every swing of his axe. He fell to the ground, swinging his weapon with barely any strength. She had to help him, but how? Would her gun even help? She raised it and peered down the sights, aiming for vital areas. She pulled the trigger.

The echoing boom of gun shots reverberated through the air.

She fired more rounds, her ears ringing. Ignoring the high-pitched whine and pounding headache, she shot off some more. Determined. Her bullets were helping. The ones who were too slow for the gun fell down in a heap. She was keeping them off Finn.

Another scream tore through the air. Alex was bitten, too. Still, he fought off the creatures. Even wounded, he was a force to be reckoned with. He didn't need help. He thrust his dagger with small, effective strikes to kill areas—a stab through the femoral artery, a neck swipe, a blade to the gut.

Good. He was okay.

She turned her attention back to Finn. He was lying on the ground now. Jari was close by, swinging her katanas in deadly fast strikes through the air. She jumped onto a mound of bodies, burying her blade in a creature. She ripped it out again and jumped off the pile, landing, rolling, and swiping two more in the backs of their knees. They collapsed with a grunt. She paid them no mind, swiping and stabbing through more creatures, defending Finn with every bit of strength she had.

Lir cried out. Mya whipped her head around and watched as he sliced through his attacker. The Vrykolaka fell to the ground without its head. Blood dripped from a wound in Lir's neck.

Mya struggled to think of how she could help all of them. What could she do? She already called the night and the shadows. She sifted through her mind, trying to remember what Hecate said. She could use the moon for power, but how? What could she do with it? That was no use. She needed something *now!* She could affect their dreams, but that was fucking useless in this fight.

What was the other thing . . . ?

She could make them go to sleep! But there were hundreds of them left. Could she make all of them slumber?

Mya thought about what it meant to be asleep. Forcing that state into her mind, she raised her arms and urged that feeling toward the monsters. But nothing happened. Struggling now, she focused everything she had into her mind.

Sleep! she mentally commanded. Sweat poured down her face as she shouted the command again. *Sleep!*

The Vrykolakas fell to the ground in a boneless heap, their eyes rolling back into their heads. Some of them even snored. The witches dropped their barrier. The gods lay on the ground, eyes wide as they watched the monsters snoozing.

Jari ran to her. "Are you okay?" She slid her hands over Mya's body, checking for injuries.

"I'm fine," she said. "I don't need a body check. None of them got to me. I'm sure Lir, o master protector, had a hand in that one."

Jari ignored her, squeezing her into a hug. "Let's get these guys home. They need to heal."

Mya looked around. Aiden, Alex, Lir, and Finn were all on the ground, injured and weak.

"Agreed," she said.

Hecate appeared out of thin air.

Alex growled at her. Raising his body off the ground, he limped to her. "You fucking *bitch!* Where were you?"

Hecate crossed her arms and glared. "My powers are useless in this fight. You'll have to forgive me for choosing to live! I stayed close by, ready to extract if needed."

"Powers are useless? Are you not a goddamn goddess of magic!"

She stepped closer to him and spoke with anger in her voice. "Of course I am, but I don't kill with my magic, you idiot!"

"And why the hell not?" He took a step closer to her.

"The kind of magic required to kill someone is called black magic. Would you like me to spell that out for you, you imbecile?" Not waiting for his rebuff, she continued. "If a witch of my caliber dabbles in corrupt black magic, you can kiss everything you know goodbye. I would be a power this universe has never seen before."

"Humble, too. Wonderful," he said.

"It is a fact!" she yelled into his face. They were now inches apart. "Besides, I came back to help all of you heal and get out of here." She looked at the witches. "Will you clean up this mess for us regarding the police?"

They nodded, though they were all shaking and pale.

Lir stood up from where he sat against a tree. "No need to clean up." He raised his arms, calling the sea.

The water flooded the park with seawater, but ignored Mya. It wrapped around her gently before receding back into the ocean, taking the sleeping creatures with it. Mya wasn't sure how to feel about that. Killing them when they were asleep and unable to defend themselves felt wrong, but the Vrykolakas would've killed them otherwise.

Jari leaned into her. "They can't die from drowning. Lir just bought us time to escape and rest."

She leaned her head on Jari's shoulder.

Jari smiled down at her. "Let's get you home."

Mya looked around at her new family. Home. Something she'd never experienced before. And it had only taken becoming a goddess to find her place.

ACKNOWLEDGMENTS

I'm not quite sure where to begin with this. There are so many people who helped me achieve my lifelong dream of writing my own novel, and I did it! This has been one incredible journey that I will never forget.

First, I want to thank my friend, Jacque, who was the first person to read this book. She not only helped me develop this, but added some fabulous content as well. Second, I want to thank my husband for supporting me and pretending to listen to me ramble on about my books for an entire year (maybe more). I also want to thank my children for allowing me to ignore them (sort of) while I wrote, rewrote, and edited this book. I want to thank Writer's Island, my go to writing community. You guys have taught me so much and helped me hone this novel into something even better with your invaluable talents and skills.

Last, but not least, I want to thank my readers! Without my readers, none of this would have been possible. You guys are the reason I wrote this novel, and I hope you will continue to read all my novels in the future. Please don't forget to leave an honest review so I know what you guys want to see me write in the future. I especially want to give a shout out to my beta readers who read this book at its many different stages and who gave me valuable input.

To my critique partner, Lauren Biel, you get your own special line for all the hard work you put into this with me. When I felt down about my writing, you were there for me.

lifting me up. You helped me in so many indescribable ways. I couldn't have finished this novel to the best of my ability without you!

Make sure to turn the page for a special preview of my second installment of The Guardians of Terra Series!

BOOK TWO

Mya stood on the lawn in the quiet suburban neighborhood. It felt surreal after the events of the night. Everything was too calm.

A man appeared out of the darkness. His long black hair, equally black eyes, chiseled jaw, and muscled body said he was one of them—a god. He looked at her with a predatory smile and menace behind his dark eyes.

"Hello, wife."

ABOUT THE AUTHOR

R.N. Gosser first found her love of writing through her intense love of reading. She devours stories—the more the better. She loves to read fantasy, horror, and paranormal fiction. She enjoys writing stories that are a mixture of all three genres, with a generous dose of humor. When she isn't busy writing or reading stories, she's taking care of her four children. She lives in Henderson, NV with her husband, kids, and pets. Her dream is to be a successful author.

f ⊙

Made in the USA
Monee, IL
11 August 2023